Heartland
Christmas
BRIDES

Heartland
Christmas
BRIDES

Four Historical
Christmas Romances
from the Heart of America

BARBOUR BOOKS
An Imprint of Barbour Publishing, Inc.

Print ISBN 978-1-63058-934-9

Published by Barbour Books, an imprint of Barbour
Publishing, Inc., P.O. Box 719, Uhrichsville, Ohio 44683,
www.barbourbooks.com

*Our mission is to publish and distribute inspirational products
offering exceptional value and biblical encouragement to the masses.*

 Member of the
Evangelical Christian
Publishers Association

Printed in the United States of America.

The Nutcracker Bride

by Margaret Brownley

Be not forgetful to entertain strangers:
for thereby some have entertained angels unawares.
HEBREWS 13:2

Chapter 1

Kansas, 1880

Thunderous hoofbeats broke the silence on that gray December day. Even the air crackled with urgency.

Lucy Langdon dumped a handful of hulled nuts into her bucket and looked up from beneath the walnut tree. Someone was in a big hurry. Such haste generally meant an emergency: a tornado, prairie fire, or locust invasion—a doctor needed. Or maybe Mr. Jones had been attacked by one of his chickens again.

She craned her neck, but the road curved around the Holbrook orchard, preventing her from seeing much beyond the bend.

Even her sorrel, hitched to the wagon, sensed something amiss. Ears pricked forward, she pawed the ground and whinnied.

"It's all right, Penny," Lucy called as she hastened to calm her skittish mare. As the pounding hooves moved closer, Penny tried pulling free from the traces. In the struggle to contain her horse, Lucy's straw bonnet flew off.

A shiny black steed sprang into view and galloped at full speed toward her. The horseman reined in next to her wagon, his powerful mount rearing back on its hind legs and pawing the air. A flash of blue eyes and a handsome square face greeted her from beneath his wide-brimmed hat.

"Save that for me!" the stranger yelled, spinning his mount around in a tight circle beside the wagon.

Startled, she called back, "Save what?" But her question went unanswered, for already the man had raced away.

No sooner had he vanished than three more horsemen rode into view, their faces half-hidden by scarlet kerchiefs. A shiver of panic raced through her. Outlaws!

Lucy released Penny and grabbed her shotgun from the back of the wagon. Her rapid heartbeats all but drowned out the pounding of hooves as the desperados raced past.

Paying her no heed, the masked men headed in the direction of her house. Her first thought was for her grandfather. *God, please don't let them stop there!*

She swooped up her bonnet, reached for the bucket, and tossed them into the wagon along with her shotgun. She would have to pay old man Holbrook later for the nuts.

Scrambling onto the driver's seat, she grabbed the reins and released the brake. "Gid-up!" she shouted. Cracking her whip, she drove home helter-skelter, the wheels of her wagon kicking up dust in her wake.

◦◦◦

Less than twenty minutes later, Lucy ran into her house, calling out to her neighbor. "Mrs. Abernathy! Mrs. Abernathy!"

The older woman looked up from her needlepoint, her spectacles slipping down her nose. "Good heavens, child. Why are you yelling? You'll wake your grandfather, if you haven't already."

Lucy locked the door and ran around checking all the windows. It wasn't like her to lose her ladylike composure, but this was an emergency.

"You won't believe what happened—" She talked so fast her tongue tripped over her words. On and on she went. "—and then he said, 'Save that for me' and—"

Mrs. Abernathy stared at her with rounded eyes. "Are you saying that a handsome black horse stole your nuts?"

Lucy drew her gaze from the window. "What?"

"I was asking about the handsome horse that stole your nuts."

"The man was handsome, not the horse. And the robbers—"

"My word. Did you say robbers? Are you all right, child?"

"I'm fine." Lucy collapsed in a chair and pulled off her bonnet. She wished she could say the same for the stranger on the black steed. Three against one; that wasn't very good odds by anyone's count.

Mrs. Abernathy looked visibly shaken, and Lucy felt bad for worrying her. "The highwaymen are probably gone by now," she said, sounding more confident than she felt.

"I certainly hope you're right."

In an effort to ease her neighbor's mind, Lucy changed the subject. "Did Grandfather give you any trouble?" What would she do without this kindhearted neighbor's help? Mrs. Abernathy sat with Opa every Wednesday while Lucy drove into town for supplies and to deliver baked goods to her customers.

Lucy's tactic worked, and Mrs. Abernathy's worried frown faded away. "Your grandfather is a love. He and I had a nice chat about old times."

"A nice chat" meant Mrs. Abernathy had done all the talking. The only word Grandfather had uttered in more than two years was his late wife's name. Mrs. Abernathy probably preferred his silence. She never could understand his German accent, which had remained as thick as the day he landed in America thirty-five years earlier.

Mrs. Abernathy gathered up her sewing. "I better take these old bones home, dear."

"Maybe you should wait." The bandits were probably gone, but it never paid to take chances.

"I only have a mile to go. Besides, what would a robber do with an old lady like me? The only things I own of any value are my wedding ring and the family Bible."

After donning her woolen shawl, gloves, and hat, Mrs. Abernathy reached for her sewing basket. She was round as a barrel and waddled as she walked to the door.

"I wish you would reconsider," Lucy said.

Mrs. Abernathy patted her on the arm. "It's better that I go now while it's still light and before it begins to snow."

Lucy kissed her on a parched cheek. The old woman smelled like violets and cloves. "Be careful and don't forget your pastries." She handed Mrs. Abernathy a tin of her special fruit and nut Christmas cakes.

The woman chuckled. "Harold would never forgive me if I did."

Lucy followed her outside to the horse and wagon

parked in front. The road was deserted, and a cold wind cut through her woolen skirt. A strand of coppery hair pulled free from her bun, and she brushed it away from her face.

"Take care."

"Don't you go worryin' none, you hear? You have enough troubles as it is." Mrs. Abernathy climbed onto the seat of her wagon. "I wish you would let me watch him on Sunday so you could go to meeting." Nobody in town went to "church." It was always "go to meeting," a phrase left over from the days the town had no church and worship was held in private homes.

"It's kind of you to offer, but I wouldn't feel right keeping you from worshipping with your husband."

Mrs. Abernathy discounted her concern with a flutter of her hand. "Harold wouldn't mind, long as you don't wake him when he falls asleep. The reverend believes that 'life everlasting' refers to the length of the sermon." She chuckled as she gathered the reins in her hands. "I just hope that handsome horse returns with your walnuts."

The memory of blue eyes flashed through Lucy's mind. "I do, too," she said, and laughed. Hugging herself for warmth, she watched until the back of her neighbor's wagon vanished behind a wall of gray haze.

A few snowflakes began to fall. Winter was here at last. Turning toward the house with a shiver, Lucy caught a glimpse of her grandfather wandering about the yard dressed only in his red long johns. Oh no, not again!

Lately, all he wanted was to escape outside. . .searching, always searching for Eva, her dear, deceased grandmother and his beloved wife.

Chiding herself for not closing the door all the way, she hastened across the yard. Just before leading him back inside, she glanced at the dark, angry sky, and a feeling of foreboding washed over her.

Chapter 2

Good intentions to the contrary, Lucy sat on tenterhooks the rest of the day. The brave front she'd managed for Mrs. Abernathy's benefit had long since deserted her.

The narrow dirt road was deserted, but that didn't keep her from flying to the parlor window every few minutes in search of lurkers. She'd posted signs on the wooden fence in front of her property, warning any passersby to watch for outlaws.

Sensing her anxiety, her grandfather seemed especially restless. Every time she turned her back, he made a beeline for the front door.

She pulled him away for perhaps the tenth or eleventh time. "You don't want to go outside, Opa," she explained patiently. "It's cold." He'd always insisted she call him Opa, the German word for grandfather.

"Don't worry," she added for her own benefit. "The thieves are probably miles away by now." She didn't want to think about what might have happened to the

man on the black steed. She only hoped his commanding presence was enough to save him.

She seated her grandfather on a chair in front of the
blazing fire. The doctor had a term for Opa's condition,
which she refused to embrace. She didn't know why a
kind and loving man had, through the years, become
an empty shell, but she refused to believe him insane.

How much he heard or understood, she couldn't
guess, but talking to him helped her feel better. At
least it made the silence bearable, though it did little to
abate the loneliness.

"Stay here and I'll get our supper, Opa." She had
made his favorite lamb stew, and the delicious smell
wafting into the parlor made her mouth water.

She walked into the kitchen and grabbed an apron.
Orders for her baked goods were stacked on the counter
next to her recipe file and notebook. The numbers
assured her that it would be a merry Christmas indeed.
With the money left over after living expenses, she
would finally be able to hire someone to make much-
needed repairs on the sod house and barn.

The house had been built by her grandfather's own
hands thirty years earlier. He'd cut the sod into blocks,
sawed cottonwood for rafters, and made the wooden
roof shingles by hand.

Through the years, additional rooms had been added as needed, like tiles in a game of dominoes. Now they had the luxury of three bedrooms. But the kitchen remained her favorite place. Not only did it remind her of the many happy hours spent learning the baking trade at her grandmother's side, but the process of sifting flour and cracking nuts offered a welcome respite from her troubles.

She set to work at once, pulling ingredients from her pantry. Dumplings would go nicely with the stew. She reached for the bag of flour and found the shelf empty. It was then that she remembered leaving her groceries and walnuts in the back of the wagon. She'd been so upset by her earlier encounter, she'd unharnessed the horse but had forgotten to unload.

Donning her shawl, she left the house quietly, hoping her grandfather wouldn't try to follow. It was still light enough to see her way to the barn without benefit of a lantern.

The wind was icy and the air hung thick with the promise of more snow. Penny greeted her in the barn with a soft neigh, and a hen clucked from its roost.

Her nuts were scattered on the bottom of the wagon, and she decided to leave them till the following day, when the light would be better. Tomorrow she would remove the hulls and start the curing process by spreading the black walnuts out to dry for next year's baking.

She reached for the crate of groceries purchased from Walden's Mercantile. As she lifted the wooden box out of the wagon, an unfamiliar gunnysack caught her attention.

"Now where did that come from?" It hadn't been there when she'd loaded her groceries. Of that she was certain.

Curious, she set the crate down and pulled the coarse cloth sack out of the wagon. Setting it on the barn floor, she released the drawstring tie, and her eyes widened in astonishment.

Heart pounding, she jerked her hand back. Had she seen what she thought she saw?

With a nervous glance around, she grabbed hold of the gunnysack and dragged it over to the open barn door where the light was brighter. This time the shock of discovery hit her full force.

The sack was full of money!

∞

Lucy stared at the stacks of banknotes spread across her kitchen table. Each bundle of hundred-dollar bills was bound with a paper band. The grand total was seventy thousand dollars. Never could she have imagined so much money in one place.

Save this for me.

The memory of the man's puzzling request triggered a disturbing thought. Perhaps she'd gotten it all wrong. Maybe the blue-eyed stranger on the black horse was also a thief. That meant. . .

Panic bubbled up inside. What if he came looking for her? There were very few houses in the area. She wouldn't be that difficult to find.

Forcing herself to breathe, Lucy tried to think. This was no time to go off the deep end. She needed a clear head to consider her options.

Riding into town to the marshal's office was out of the question. That would require taking her grandfather out in the cold. Besides, it was almost dark. And what if it started to snow or she ran into bandits on the road?

A sound from the other room made her jump. Quickly rising from her chair, she hurried to the parlor. It was just her grandfather trying to open the front door again. Thank God he hadn't yet learned how to turn the newly installed lock.

Taking him gently by the arm, she spoke in a soothing voice. "You don't want to go outside, Opa. Your supper is almost ready."

She steered him away from the door and, with an anxious glance out the front window, walked him back to his chair in front of the blazing fire. She had a feeling it was going to be a very long night.

∞

Texas Ranger Chad Prescott tugged on the reins of his black horse. "Whoa, boy."

He turned up his coat collar and stared in the direction of the house. A light shone from the window, and the smell of smoke told him a fire blazed within. He could use a bit of warmth right now. He'd been riding for hours and was colder than a Montana well digger.

After leading the notorious Dobson gang on a merry chase, he was finally able to double back. He'd planned to sneak up from behind, but somehow he lost them.

No matter. He'd find them—all three of them. He always got his man, or in this case, men. First he had to locate a certain pretty, copper-haired woman with eyes the color of a Texas bluebonnet. If he didn't retrieve the money in her possession, he'd have a lot of explaining to do.

As the night wore on, his worries increased. For a state as flat as Kansas, it didn't seem possible that people could so quickly disappear. The sooner he finished his business here and hailed back to Texas, the better.

The temperature had dropped the moment night fell. He was cold and hungry and could sure use some shut-eye. Riding back to town sounded like a good idea. He would begin his search again first thing in the morning.

No sooner had he made the decision than he heard something flapping against the fence that ran parallel to the road. A closer look revealed some sort of sign. He dismounted and pulled a box of safety matches out of his saddlebag. His back against the wind, he lit a match, cupping his hand around the flame.

He was able to pick out the word "bandits" before the match went out. His mouth curved upward as he pulled the sign down and stuffed it in his pocket. Well now. Looka there. A certain young woman had sounded the alarm. Unless he was mistaken, he was standing in front of her house.

As tempting as it was to march up to her door and ask for the money tossed in her wagon for safekeeping, he decided to check in back first. If Frank Dobson and his brothers were hiding inside, he wanted to know about it before walking into a trap.

Chapter 3

It was late, nearly nine o'clock, before Lucy took the last batch of cookies out of the oven and set them on a rack to cool. The only time she could fill her orders uninterrupted was when her grandfather was asleep.

She'd hidden the money beneath a loose floorboard in the parlor and covered it with a rag rug. Tomorrow she would decide what to do next. Maybe she could flag down one of her neighbors and ask him to take it to the marshal. That would save her the hassle of dragging her grandfather along.

Or maybe—

Startled by a loud thud, she dropped her wooden spoon and flew to the window over the kitchen sink. It was too dark to see out, but it sure did sound like the barn door.

In all the confusion of finding the money, she must have forgotten to latch it. Penny and the other animals could freeze to death if she didn't do something.

Reaching for her shawl, she hesitated a moment

before grabbing the shotgun. After lighting a lantern, she cautiously opened the door. A blast of frigid air blew out the flame. Knowing the futility of lighting it again, she hung the lantern back on the hook.

Anxious to get the job done and return to the house before freezing her fanny off, she stepped out on the porch. The robbers still very much on her mind, she kept her finger on the trigger.

The wind whistled through the eaves, and her skirt whipped against her legs. The barn door kept up a steady rhythm, like a drummer during a death march. Stomach clenched tight and senses alert, she moved forward.

She reached the end of the porch and was just about to descend the steps when a dark form loomed in front of her.

Jumping back, Lucy's breath caught audibly in her throat and her hand jerked. A flash of light and deafening blast from her shotgun sent her reeling.

Thinking with her feet, she managed to get back inside and slam the door shut. She stared down at her weapon, and reality hit her. Dear God, what had she done? The shotgun slid from her hands and fell to the floor with a clatter.

Breathing hard, she listened. Only the moaning

wind and banging barn door could be heard over her pounding heart.

Cold fear gripped her as she walked on silent feet to the sink. Moving the curtain, she peered out the window. Seeing only the reflection of her own pale face, she dropped the curtain. Frightful images raced through her head.

A sudden pounding startled her, followed by a man's rough voice. "Open up!"

She retrieved her shotgun from the floor. "What. . . what do you want?" she called in a wavering voice.

"I need help, lady." Silence followed and then, "I've been shot."

She lowered her weapon until the muzzle pointed downward. Had she really shot him, or was it a trick? "H–how do I know you're telling the truth?"

"You'll know when you open the door." His voice sounded weaker. Maybe he really was hurt. Then again, maybe it was a trick. *God, please tell me what to do.*

"I c–can't. You might have evil intentions."

"Lady. . ." Pause. "Right now. . ." More silence. "I couldn't hurt a fly."

It sounded like he was telling the truth, but how could she be sure? Then she remembered something Opa had told her long ago. The fastest way to know a man's true character is through his relationship to God.

"Can. . .can you recite a Bible verse?"

It took so long for an answer to come, she feared the man was dead. Finally, she heard his muffled voice. "What?"

"A Bible verse." A man who knew his Bible couldn't be all bad. "What is your favorite verse? It'll help me know if I can trust you."

"Thou shalt not. . .*kill*."

She pursed her lips. "Actually, the Bible doesn't say that. It says thou shalt not *murder*." An important distinction, in her estimation. "Of course, a lot of people say 'kill' when they mean—" She was yammering on about nothing but couldn't seem to help herself. It was how she dealt with nerves. "But I'm sure God forgives—"

"Open the blasted door!"

⋙

The moment he stumbled into her kitchen, Lucy recognized him as the man on the black horse.

Blood dripped onto the floor, and he leaned heavily on her as she half dragged him to the spare bedroom. No sooner had they reached the bed than he collapsed on the straw mattress in a state of unconsciousness.

He was a large man—even larger than her

grandfather—with wide shoulders and a broad chest. He was also tall, and his feet hung over the bottom of the mattress. It took every bit of strength she possessed to roll him over so she could tend to his wound. The amount of blood alarmed her, and she feared she'd done him serious harm.

She worked frantically to pull off his coat, vest, and shirt. *Please don't let him die, God.*

Fortunately, she was no stranger to bullet wounds, thanks to her work as Doc Hathaway's assistant.

Her steady hand and sharp mind made her a quick study, but none of those other bullets had been her fault. That alone unnerved her. What if she did something wrong? What if the man died? Would that make her a murderer? *Dear God, no!*

Pushing such terrifying thoughts aside, she focused on the task at hand. She bound her patient's wound with strips of cotton fabric to stop the bleeding and hastened to the kitchen. After lighting the fire under the kettle, she searched through the kitchen drawers. The kitchen tongs were too large for pulling out a bullet, so she settled on two teaspoons.

Fortunately, the gunshot blast hadn't awakened her grandfather. The man could sleep through anything, and for that, she was grateful.

The barn door was still banging, but that would have to wait until after she'd taken care of her patient. The thought of going back outside filled her with dread, but concern for the animals took precedence over fear.

Calming her still-pounding heart, she reached into the sewing basket.

Doc Hathaway believed that unless a wound was deep, it was best to let it heal naturally. Just in case, she pulled out needle and thread. Recalling that more men had died during the War between the States from infection than bullet wounds, she grabbed a bottle of tincture of iodine.

After gathering her supplies and arranging them on a tray, along with a bottle of medicinal whiskey, she hurried to her patient's side.

She adjusted the lamp and set to work. He was still bleeding quite a bit, but as far as she could tell, the bullet hadn't penetrated any vital organs. That alone was a blessing. As long as the slug hadn't lodged in a bone, it shouldn't be that hard to remove.

With some careful probing, Lucy managed to locate the bullet in the fleshy area of the chest next to the man's armpit. It took several tries before she managed to grab hold of the pellet between the spoons and ease it out. The slug made a pinging sound as it hit the bottom of the porcelain bowl.

After packing the wound to stop the bleeding, she covered it with iodine-painted gauze and strips of clean muslin. After mopping up the blood and washing her hands, she laid a damp cloth on his forehead.

Doc Hathaway had impressed on her the importance of keeping a professional attitude at all times when treating a patient. But, God forgive her, it was hard not to notice what a handsome man this was. He had a firm, square jaw, a straight patrician nose, and a nicely shaped mouth. His manly chest wasn't bad to look at either.

Surprised and even dismayed by such unladylike thoughts, she checked his forehead for fever before slipping out of the room to take care of that barn door.

Tomorrow, if the weather permitted, she would fetch the doctor. Meanwhile, there was nothing to do but wait and pray. Oh yes, and try to maintain a professional attitude.

Chapter 4

Chad had a hard time letting go of the darkness. When at last his eyes fluttered open, it took a moment to gather his bearings. His lips were parched and his mouth as dry as the desert sands. Worse, it felt like someone was inside his head pounding with a hammer. Where was he? He blinked, and gradually his vision cleared.

It took longer for his memory to kick in. Bits and pieces dwindled back, but none made sense. He remembered pain—and then softness. He recalled thinking he was burning up. . .until a feather-light coolness touched his brow.

Blue eyes—he remembered those, too. And hair the color of a coppery Texas sun.

He tried to move, and groaned. The memories might not be real, but the pain sure was, though he had a hard time locating it.

Only a sliver of gray light filtered through the curtains. It sure didn't look like his room at Mrs.

Compton's boardinghouse. It didn't look like heaven either. For one thing, there was a row of wooden puppets staring down from a shelf, their garish painted faces mocking him.

He moved his legs and froze. His gun and boots were missing. So, for that matter, were his trousers, but that was of less concern.

He tried sitting up, but the room turned topsy-turvy. One moment the puppets were on the floor; next they were on the raftered ceiling. He fell back against the pillow. Something was wrong with his arm. His shoulder was wrapped in a bandage, and when he tried moving it, pain shot down his arm.

He grimaced, and all at once it came back to him. He'd been shot.

A sound alerted him. Footsteps. The door opened with a creak of its leather hinges. The dim light revealed a curvy feminine form.

Not till she stepped into the room could he see the woman's delicate features. Her eyes—those he remembered. How could he not? They reminded him of the bluebonnets that grew in wild abundance back home in Texas. So the angel of his dreams was real.

He moved and heard her intake of breath.

"You're awake," she said.

"Barely." He waited for her to come near the bed. She leaned over to check his bandage, and a delicate lavender scent wafted toward him. Her eyes were sharp and assessing as she probed, and only when he flinched did she pull away.

"Sorry," she said. "How do you feel?"

"Like I've been shot." He studied her, and the fog in his head cleared. "Why'd you do that? Why'd you shoot me?"

She stared at him accusingly. "You scared me."

"Not as much as you scared me."

Her eyes widened. "You shouldn't have jumped out at me like that."

He frowned. Is that what he'd done? He remembered checking her barn for her horse and wagon and, recognizing both, walking to the house. He didn't even know she was on the porch until she fired at him.

When he failed to respond, she added, "I never meant to cause you harm. My gun went off accidentally."

Since it was partly his fault, he might have let her off the hook had she looked halfway apologetic or even vulnerable. Instead, she looked like a force to be reckoned with. She held herself erect, her features composed. Her copper hair was pulled into a tight bun and her pleated shirtwaist buttoned up to her chin.

A model of prudence, modesty, and efficiency. He doubted she did anything by chance, and that might include firing a gun.

"Hard to tell the difference between an accident or good aim," he said. "I reckon they both hurt the same."

Not that he was an expert. As a Texas Ranger, he'd chased more trigger-itching outlaws than he cared to count, and not once had he taken a bullet. Being shot at was bad enough. But having his perfect record broken by a pint-sized woman who probably weighed no more than a goose-down pillow was doggone galling.

She reached for the pitcher on the table by his bedside and picked up a clean glass. Every movement was precise and unhurried. He seemed to remember her forcing liquids down his throat, for which he was grateful.

"If I scared you so much, how come you let me in the house?"

Affording him a wary glance, she filled the glass and set the pitcher down. "I asked you for a Bible verse. I figured a man able to recite Scripture couldn't be all bad."

He shook his head in wonder. The woman was either terribly naive or terribly trusting. Either way, he lucked out, or he might have bled to death on her doorstep.

"You better drink this."

His dry mouth told him it was probably good advice. He managed to pull himself upright while she fluffed his pillow with her free hand. Taking the glass from her, he gulped the water down his prickly throat and then checked his bandaged shoulder.

"The swelling has gone down," she said. "And it doesn't look quite as red."

That was good to hear. If only his head would stop pounding. "Who else lives here?"

Suspicion crossed her face and her eyes narrowed. "Why do you ask?"

He frowned. Obviously she didn't trust him. "Just want to know who took care of me."

"I did," she said.

Considering her size, that was hard to believe. "Does that mean you undressed me, too?"

She refused to meet his gaze but couldn't hide her reddening cheeks. "Your trousers and shirt were covered in blood."

"How did you get fluids down me?"

This time she looked straight at him. "With a funnel."

He thought about that for a moment. "What did the doctor say?"

She took the empty glass from him and set it on

the bedside table. "Doctor?"

"A doctor removed the bullet, right?"

"No, I did," she said.

"You?" The woman was full of surprises.

"The doctor lives an hour away, and it was snowing hard."

He clenched his teeth. Going out in the snow seemed like a small price to pay for shooting him, even if it was partly his fault. Still, judging by the feel of things, she'd done a pretty good job without a physician's help.

"How many bullets have you taken out anyway?"

"Yours was the fourth, or maybe the fifth," she said in the same straightforward tone he'd already come to expect.

He stared at her. "That many?"

"Yes, and they weren't all accidents."

"Something to keep in mind," he muttered. It was just his luck to have a run-in with a trigger-happy damsel. "Did you shoot them yourself, or did you have help?"

His question brought a shadow of a smile to her lips. "Neither. I worked as a doctor's assistant."

"Ah, that explains it," he said. "By the way, my name's Chad Prescott."

"Miss Langdon. Miss Lucy Langdon."

"How long have I been here?"

"Four days," she said.

Four! He couldn't believe his ears. Now, wasn't that just fine and dandy? That gang of outlaws he'd trailed all the way from Texas were probably long gone by now.

"What about my horse?"

"He has been well cared for and is in the barn." After a moment, she asked, "What's his name?"

"I call him Spirit."

She repeated the name, and coming from her, it sounded almost musical. "That suits him."

Anxious to get down to business, Chad tried moving his legs, but they felt like lead. "I tossed something in your wagon."

"Oh?" She busied herself smoothing the bedcovers. "I hope it was a change of clothes."

The woman was joking, right? "Not clothes. A gunnysack."

Her gaze locked with his. "Why would you do such a thing? Toss something in my wagon, I mean?"

"If you recall, I was being chased by three hombres. I didn't want them getting their hands on it."

She studied him as if to determine whether he spoke the truth. "When it stops snowing, I'll check the wagon to see if. . .your bag is still there," she said.

"Never mind. I'll check myself, if you will kindly tell me where I can find my shirt and trousers."

"Your clothes are drying in front of the fire. Like I said, they were soaked with blood, so I washed them."

"What about my gun and boots?" he asked. "Did you wash those, too?"

She lifted her gaze to his. "You won't be needing those, Mr. Prescott. At least not for a while."

He tossed the blanket away and was surprised by the effort it took to swing his legs over the side of the bed.

Looking as prim as a preacher's wife at a prayer meeting, Miss Langdon folded her arms across her chest. "You're not in any condition to walk, Mr. Prescott."

"Wanna bet?" He planted his feet firmly on the floor—or at least that's what he meant to do. Instead, he somehow landed on his knees.

She stared down at him. "Would you like me to help you back in bed?"

"Never mind. I'll do it myself." He pulled himself upright and flopped facedown across the mattress. At least the woman had the decency to let him keep the bottom of his long johns on.

"I'll fix you something to eat then." She pulled the

sheet and blanket over him. "You need to get your strength back."

He heard her leave the room and gritted his teeth. Like it or not, he wasn't going anywhere. Not for a while anyway.

Chapter 5

The following morning, Lucy pulled the baking sheet of *pfeffernüsse* out of the oven, and the sweet smell of cinnamon and cloves filled the air. Nudging the bowl of freshly cracked nuts and the tall wooden nutcracker aside, she set the metal sheet on the counter. She then sprinkled the cookies with spiced sugar.

The cookie recipe had been handed down by her German grandmother, who got it from her grandmother. After the cookies cooled, Lucy would pack them into tins to distribute to her customers.

A blizzard had raged for three days, piling drifts against the house and barn. The only person to come to her door in all that time was dear old Mr. Abernathy to check up on her. She made no mention of her guest. It would only worry him and his wife.

She hoped it would stop snowing long enough to allow her to make deliveries. If she could reach the Brookstone farm down the road a ways, perhaps they would let her use their sleigh.

She reached for another baking sheet and turned toward the oven. Just then the back door sprang open. Startled, she dropped the tray, and cookie dough spattered across the floor.

"Mr. Prescott!" Her mouth fell open. Never had she seen such a frightful sight. His bare feet were red, and his uncombed hair and unshaven chin were peppered with fresh-fallen snow. Over his long johns he wore one of Opa's shirts.

"You nearly scared the life out of me," she scolded. The shirt barely stretched across his massive shoulders and allowed for an intriguing glimpse of his broad, muscular chest. Much to her annoyance, she felt her cheeks blaze.

He slammed the door shut behind him, his face livid. "Where is it?"

"Please keep your voice down. My grandfather—"

"Where is it?" he asked again, advancing toward her with a menacing look.

Refusing to be intimidated, she lifted her chin. "Where is what?"

He stopped a few feet in front of her. "The bag I tossed in your wagon."

The more she felt herself wilt beneath his angry gaze, the more determined she was not to back down.

"I don't know what you're talking about."

"I don't believe you."

He took another step forward, and she leaned back. "I–It's the truth," she stammered. She hated lying, but she had no intention of turning the money over to anyone but the sheriff.

Trapped by the counter behind her, Lucy felt for the wooden nutcracker. But before she could reach it, Mr. Prescott grabbed her arm. Yanking her toward him, his bare chest pressed against her.

"I'll ask you one more time. What did you do with the bag?"

She glared up at him. "I don't know what you're talking about."

Suddenly, he released her, and a pensive look crossed his face. "What's your favorite Bible verse?" he asked.

So now he was playing her game. "Thou shalt not steal!"

He laughed. "So you think I'm a thief, do you?"

"Are you?"

Just as he started to reply, her grandfather shuffled into the room. Mr. Prescott hesitated a moment before turning and leaving the kitchen.

∽

Lucy was so shaken by the encounter with Mr. Prescott, she almost didn't hear her grandfather at the front door later that morning. Rushing into the parlor, she grabbed him firmly but gently by the arm.

"Eva," he murmured. "Eva."

"Eva's not out there, Opa," she said. How could she make her grandfather understand that his wife was not coming back? She opened the door, and wind-driven snow blew inside. "Brrr." She closed the door. "You don't want to go out there."

Never had she known her grandfather to be so restless. His determination to escape these last couple of days had exhausted her. Was Mr. Prescott's presence causing Opa's distress? Or was his condition growing worse?

"Come along." She drew him away from the door and helped him into his chair. Tossing another log onto the fire, she then wrapped a knitted shawl around his thin shoulders.

Intent on making him as comfortable as possible, she failed to notice Mr. Prescott's presence until he spoke.

"What's wrong with him?" he asked.

She looked up to where he stood in the kitchen doorway, his long, lean form propped against the wooden frame. He had shaved with the razor she set out for him, and his smooth jaw emphasized his good looks, as did his neatly combed hair. Despite his uncommon dress, he exuded a powerful presence, but it was the sudden change in demeanor that disarmed her. He looked genuinely concerned, with none of his earlier rancor.

"The doctor says he's lost his mind."

He studied her. "What do you think?"

"I think his mind is still there. It's just locked inside."

He broke away from the doorway. "And you take care of him all by yourself?"

She nodded. "I'm the only family he has left." Her father had died in 1858 during the Kansas Border War when Lucy was only three. The news of his death sent her expectant mother into labor, which neither she nor her unborn baby survived. Had her grandparents not taken Lucy into their hearts and home, she would have ended up in an orphanage. Now she returned the favor by caring for her dear, sweet grandfather.

Mr. Prescott sat on an upholstered chair. "It must be hard on you."

Heaving a sigh, Lucy dropped to her knees to check the clothes drying next to the fire. "It's getting harder. My grandmother died this past summer. I don't know why, but lately Grandfather keeps trying to leave the house to search for her. He thinks she's outside."

"Why would he think that?"

"The last time he saw her alive was when she walked out that door." Her grandmother had driven into town on that fatal day and never returned. "The doctor said it was her heart."

"I'm sorry," he said.

Observing him through lowered lashes, she moistened her lips. "Your shirt is dry, but I'm afraid your trousers and coat are still damp." The heavy wool fabric took forever to dry.

Her fingers touched his as she handed him the shirt, and she quickly pulled her hand away. He yanked off her grandfather's shirt and tossed it aside. Next to the white bandage at his shoulder, his bare chest looked as golden brown as tanned leather.

Confused by the way he affected her, Lucy quickly turned to the hearth and reached for the poker. As if to free herself of his mesmerizing hold, she stabbed at the burning log until sparks flew up the chimney.

"You can look now," he said, and she detected a note of amusement in his voice.

Replacing the poker, she transferred her gaze to him. His shirt was securely buttoned, and relief flooded through her.

He sat forward on the chair, hands clasped between his knees. "I'm afraid we got off to a bad start."

She tried to maintain the impersonal and professional demeanor she'd learned from the doctor. "You have been rather difficult," she said, her voice cool and precise.

"Actually, I was referring to the bullet you pumped into me."

She faltered in her efforts to remain aloof. "I hope you find it in your heart to forgive me." As it was, she was having a hard time forgiving herself. She was lucky her carelessness hadn't done more damage.

"Yes, well. . ." He rubbed his hands together. "I'm willing to let bygones be bygones. That is, providing you come clean and tell me what happened to the gunnysack I tossed in your wagon."

She sat back on her heels. "I have no idea what you're talking about."

"I think you do, but we'll get to that in a minute. First, I think you should know that I'm a Texas Ranger, and I've been trailing a gang of outlaws for weeks. Followed them clear up here from the Panhandle."

Lucy frowned. Could he be telling the truth? "That's a long way to travel."

"I reckon I'll wear out another saddle or two before

I'm done." His face hardened, but his eyes filled with pain. Not physical pain, but something deeper and more private. "There are three of them, and they killed my best friend. Shot him in the back."

"How awful for you," she whispered, speaking from the heart. "I'm so sorry."

"Thanks." He blew out his breath. "I'm out for justice, and until I get it. . ." He shrugged. "I guess you could say I have a one-track mind."

He looked and sounded sincere, but she was still hesitant to believe him. "Don't you rangers have to wear a badge or something?"

"What?"

"A badge. Nothing on your person led me to believe you were a lawman."

"The Texas Rangers don't wear badges. Not unless we make them ourselves. A few made badges out of Mexican coins, but I never did. Never saw a need. I figured my warrant of authority was enough."

"And where is your warrant of authority now, Mr. Prescott?"

"At the boardinghouse where I've been staying," he said.

A likely story. . . Or was it? "And the bag you claim you tossed in my wagon?"

"I surprised the gang while they were robbing a stage. They dropped it and I grabbed it."

His story sounded plausible, but what if he was a crook? What if he was only trying to trick her into revealing the whereabouts of the stolen money?

"There's really no way for me to know that you're telling the truth," she said.

He rubbed the back of his neck. "Guess not, ma'am. That kind of puts us in the same boat, doesn't it?"

"How do you mean?"

He locked her gaze in his. "You told me you know nothing about the bag I left in your wagon. Now either you're lying or you're not. No way for me to know, is there?"

She hesitated, torn by conflicting emotions. She wanted to believe him, she did. But something held her back. "Has it ever occurred to you that perhaps those three bandits might have found it?"

He stared her square in the eye. "No ma'am. That never occurred to me."

She smiled. "Well then." She rose to signal that their discussion was over. "Mystery solved."

Chapter 6

Chad spent the rest of the morning conducting a thorough search of the premises.

For the most part, Miss Langdon ignored him. Though he noticed her mouth grew tighter as he pawed his way through the kitchen cupboards. Wire whisk in hand, she never said a word when he started on the pantry, but whatever was in that bowl of hers took a terrible beating.

"Aha!" he crowed upon finding his holstered gun on a shelf next to a sack of flour.

He found his boots stashed behind the butter churn.

He worked his way meticulously through the house, room by room and inch by inch. Not till he reached the lady's chamber did she react.

"Mr. Prescott!" She came charging into the room after him, looking as indignant as a newly shorn sheep. "You've gone too far this time."

"Now don't go off half-cocked," he said.

For some reason, this only seemed to incense her

more. Eyes flashing, she tossed her head, and her chest rose and fell like angry waves.

"I have never gone off half-cocked in my life. But you have no right going through my personal belongings."

He bent over her until his nose practically touched hers. "And you have no right keeping that money from me."

Glowering, she tightened her hands into fists. "You won't find any money here."

"I guess you won't mind my looking then." He straightened. "Unless you have something to hide."

She clenched her teeth and seethed with rage. "I have to say, Mr. Prescott, you are the most annoying man I've ever met."

"And you, Miss Langdon, are the most annoying woman." Though he had to admit, she sure did make outrage look enticing. "Now that we've found something we can agree on, you'll have to excuse me while I continue my search."

"Don't let me stop you!" She left the room, slamming the door so hard a picture fell off the wall.

Grinning, he picked up the picture. The lady was a force to be reckoned with, that's for sure. Better watch his step. The last thing he needed was another bullet wound.

He glanced about the tidy room and decided to start the search with the large wooden chest at the foot of the bed.

He lifted the lid and got the shock of his life. A stack of satin and lace under-riggins—the likes of which he had never seen—greeted his startled eyes. Hers? Were they really hers? And if so, what was an unmarried woman doing with a chest full of apparel more likely to be found in a bordello than a farmhouse?

He hesitated before plunging his hands into the provocative depths. It felt wrong pawing through such personal attire, but a lot of money was at stake—money for which he was responsible.

The sheer femininity of the corsets, petticoats, and camisoles was enough to make even the most jaded man blush. As it was, he had trouble breathing as he rummaged through the feminine finery.

Finding no gunnysack, he pulled back and lowered the lid, but that did nothing to quell his wayward thoughts.

Well, now. What do you know? The lady wasn't quite as straitlaced as she'd led him to believe. What else didn't he know about her?

⁓

It was 11:00 p.m., and Lucy was exhausted. Not only had her grandfather worn her to a frazzle by constantly trying to escape, but Mr. Prescott's disturbing presence made her feel—what? Anxious? Nervous? Confused?

Whatever it was, he had somehow aroused a womanly response that was all at once frightening and exciting. Never had a man affected her more.

Banishing such thoughts, she stifled a yawn and glanced around the kitchen. Dirty dishes were still stacked on the counter, but that was the least of it. She still had nuts to crack and flour to sift and butter to melt and. . .

Feeling overwhelmed, she sank onto a chair. She folded her arms on the kitchen table and laid her head down. If only Grandmother hadn't died. If only Opa could somehow miraculously return to his former fun-loving self. If only. . .

She groaned. How she hated feeling sorry for herself, but she couldn't seem to help it. Her grandmother had taken care of Opa when she was alive, and not once had she complained.

Lucy could still hear her grandmother's voice admonishing her not to act sad around her grandfather. *The Bible says a cheerful heart is good medicine.*

It wasn't until after Grandmother's death that Lucy found out the amount of work involved in Opa's care. Poor Oma. Is that why her heart had given out? From the strain of taking care of her husband? It was possible. And now the job had fallen squarely on Lucy's shoulders.

No matter how hard she tried to shoulder the responsibility of her grandfather's care with a loving spirit, she couldn't help but feel resentful. While her friends enjoyed barn dances, sewing bees, and socials, she was stuck at home with her silent and helpless grandfather.

To make matters worse, she was always behind schedule and barely had a moment to herself. Except for her daily Bible reading, she couldn't remember the last time she'd read a book or chatted with friends her own age.

To save time, she'd stopped shaving her grandfather, and he now sported a white beard. He would probably benefit from a bath, but he was unsteady on his feet, and she didn't want to take a chance on him falling. Sponging him off daily with hot water and soap was the most she could manage.

She wiped a damp strand of hair away from her face with the back of her hand. To make matters worse, she was behind in her orders.

Had God deserted her? It certainly felt like it, but He wasn't the only one. That awful Jason Mills sure did desert her last spring when she told him she wouldn't marry him unless he promised to care for her aging grandparents. Well, good riddance! All she had to show for a year-long courtship was the carefully sewn trousseau in her hope chest.

She sighed. What a mess. Not only had she nearly killed Mr. Prescott, but she now had seventy thousand dollars of stolen money hidden away. With a blizzard raging outside, there was little chance of riding into town anytime soon. If the weather didn't clear, she wasn't even certain she could deliver her orders in time for Christmas.

Where are you, God? And how much longer do you think I can hold on?

co

It was late, and still Chad couldn't sleep. Outside a blizzard raged as he applied a new bandage to his wound. The windows rattled and the shutters banged. By the sound of it, he wasn't going anywhere soon.

Had the Dobson gang found the money in the wagon as Miss Langdon suggested? It was possible but highly unlikely. Still, he'd searched the house high and low and had come up empty-handed.

He'd also searched the barn. Maybe she'd buried it. If so, there wasn't much he could do about it. Not with the storm raging outside and the snow piled high.

Maybe he'd handled the lady all wrong. Perhaps he should try appealing to her softer side. Now that he knew she had a softer side. . .

No sooner had the thought occurred to him than a vision of silk corsets and lace petticoats came to mind. God forgive him, but he hadn't been able to stop thinking about Miss Langdon and all that silken frippery since finding it stashed in that wooden chest. It was almost as if he'd been given a peek into the deepest regions of the lady's heart.

Surprised by his fanciful thoughts, he shook his head. He'd been cooped up too long. It was the only explanation he could think of to explain this sudden obsession with his hostess. What had it been? Five or six days? Yep, that explained it. He had cabin fever.

He was just about ready to undress for bed when something caught his ear. Crossing the room, he cracked open the door.

Was that Miss Langdon crying?

Chapter 7

At the sound of Mr. Prescott's footsteps, Lucy quickly wiped away her tears. What was he doing up at this hour of night? Couldn't a woman succumb to a moment of self-pity in privacy?

He stepped into the kitchen, fully dressed. "You all right, ma'am?" he asked, his voice edged in concern.

Lifting her chin, Lucy cleared her throat. She was certain her eyes were red and her face splotchy, but there was nothing she could do about it.

"I'm perfectly fine. Thank you."

"I thought I heard—" A look of bewilderment replaced his usual swagger. Outlaws didn't seem to faze him, but a woman in distress apparently put him in a state of confusion.

"Uh. . ." He raked his hair with his fingers. "Something smells good," he said at last.

"I'm making *zimt makronen*," she said, grateful for the change of subject. "Almond cookies."

An awkward silence followed. She tried to act like

she hadn't been crying, and he pretended not to notice her tearstained cheeks.

Finally, he cleared his throat. "Like I said. The tears. . .uh. . .cookies sure do smell good."

"Would you care to sample one?"

"If it's not too much bother."

Grateful for an excuse to escape his scrutiny, she left her seat. "Not at all."

He pulled out a chair and sat while she fixed two cups of tea and arranged the freshly baked cookies on a plate.

He picked up a carved wooden king and moved the handle on its back up and down. "What's with all the puppets?" he asked.

"They're not puppets. They're nutcrackers." She set the plate of cookies on the table and sat down. "My grandfather made them and my grandmother painted them."

He set the colorful monarch upright and helped himself to a cookie. "Never saw nutcrackers like that," he said.

"My grandfather learned the trade as a young man in Germany. Poor villagers enjoyed giving kings and other figures of authority the menial task of cracking nuts."

He chuckled. "I can see where they might."

"Unfortunately, Americans didn't have the same regard for his craft. After coming to this country, his business failed, leaving dozens of nutcrackers unsold." With a family to support, Opa had turned to farming.

"Only dozens?" he asked.

She smiled. "It does seem like more, doesn't it?" She pointed to the windowsill where several nutcrackers faced outward, including her grandmother's treasured nutcracker bride.

"It's a German tradition to keep a nutcracker in the window to protect the house from danger."

He rubbed his injured shoulder. "But not visitors?"

Her cheeks grew warm under the heat of his gaze. "Only certain ones," she said.

He bit into the cookie. "Hmm. Can't remember tasting anything this good."

She sighed and tossed a nod at the stack of tins waiting to be delivered. "I just hope I'll be able to deliver all these before Christmas. But if this storm continues—"

He dumped a spoonful of sugar in his tea and stirred. "It must be hard taking care of your grandfather and running a business."

Maybe it was his kind words or sympathetic look.

Or perhaps she was just tired, but much to Lucy's dismay she burst into tears.

A look of sheer horror crossed his face. "I'm sorry, ma'am. Never meant to upset you." He dug into his pocket and handed her a clean handkerchief.

"You didn't upset me. It's just. . ." She dabbed at her wet cheeks. "I'm not complaining, mind you. The orders are a blessing. But running a bakery and taking care of the farm and animals, I'm afraid poor Grandfather"—she was practically sobbing—"hasn't had a bath in weeks."

A combination of relief and puzzlement crossed his face. "Is that all that's got you riled?"

She blinked. "All?"

"Don't mean to make light of your troubles, ma'am, but it's been my experience that women put more stock in baths than do men. As for the other problem. . . I'll be happy to help you with deliveries. My shoulder isn't fully healed, but I'm getting stronger every day."

"That's very kind of you to offer, Mr. Prescott, but I couldn't let you go out in this weather."

"Chad," he said. "Call me Chad."

She stared at him. He really did have nice eyes, and now that she thought about it, a nice honest face as well. "I'm afraid that under the circumstances that wouldn't be proper."

He looked at her askance. "What circumstances are those?"

"Grandfather is rather old-fashioned, and since you're staying under our roof—"

He rubbed the back of his neck. "I hope you don't take this the wrong way, ma'am, but I don't think your grandfather cares one way or the other what you call me."

"Perhaps not. But on the outside chance that he does, I would prefer it if we kept things proper between us."

He thought about that for a long moment. He took a sip of his tea and thought about it some more. "By proper, does that mean I can't kiss you?"

"Mr. Prescott!"

He rose from the chair. "Just thought I'd ask. Don't want to do anything to offend your grandfather." Grabbing a handful of cookies, he left the room, whistling.

She stared after him. Her heart hammered against her ribs, and fire seemed to race though her veins. Of all the nerve—

The very thought of kissing Mr. Prescott was...what? Alarming? Shocking? *Intriguing?* Surprised by the last thought, her fingers flew to her mouth just in time to cover a most unladylike titter.

Chapter 8

The next morning, Lucy woke to the sound of a dying bull. It was only after she slipped out of bed and put her ear to the door that she was able to identify the ungodly howl as Mr. Prescott singing. Glancing at the mechanical clock, she was surprised—shocked, really—to discover she had overslept.

It was still snowing hard, and no visitors were expected in such weather. Still, she took special pains with her morning ablutions. After brushing her hair until it shone, she pinned it into a neat bun and finger-fluffed her bangs.

It took forever to decide between the blue woolen dress that matched her eyes or the pretty pink one that showed off her tiny waist. Finally, she settled on the blue.

Pinching her cheeks and moistening her lips, she left her room and entered the parlor voice first. "Must you make such a dreadful—?"

She stopped midstep. A chair had been removed

from in front of the blazing fire and the metal bathtub put in its place. Her grandfather sat in the tub, with water up to his armpits and looking perfectly content.

Speechless, Lucy lifted her gaze to Mr. Prescott, who was singing a most improper ditty about drunken sailors. Stripped from the waist up except for the bandage, he poured water into the tub from a kettle. He was soaked, and damp hair fell over his brow. His gaze suddenly fell on her, and he stopped singing.

"You're giving him a bath?" She felt something tug at her heart. "I—I don't know what to say. Except. . .it's hard to know which of you is wetter."

He set the empty kettle on the hearth. "Bathing your grandfather is harder than bathing a cow."

"You bathe cows, Mr. Prescott?"

He grinned, and her heart did a flip-flop. "Only when necessary."

Recalling his last words to her the night before, she felt her face redden. She backed out of the room. "I—I guess he's in good hands."

"At least one good hand," Mr. Prescott said, gesturing to his shoulder.

Lucy escaped to the kitchen and got another shock. Mr. Prescott had done the dishes she'd been too tired to tackle the night before. For the second time in two days, she broke down and cried.

∽

By the time Mr. Prescott joined her in the kitchen fully dressed, Lucy was busy decorating a batch of gingerbread men.

She felt oddly shy in his presence and not at all like herself. No matter how much she tried to maintain her composure, he managed to weaken her defenses.

"It was a kind thing you did," she said.

"Gotta do something to earn my keep," he replied, helping himself to one of the newly baked cookies.

His gaze clung to hers for a moment before they both looked away. She bent over to pipe eyes and mouth onto a gingerbread face, and he examined the nutcrackers guarding the window.

"This one is different." He lifted the white one off the sill and turned it over in his hands. "It looks like a bride."

She straightened, pastry bag in hand. "It *is* a bride," she said. "My grandfather gave it to my grandmother on the day he proposed marriage."

"And she still married him?" he asked with a smile.

"Why wouldn't she?"

"Most women would expect a ring," he said.

"It's a family tradition. A man places a nutcracker

bride in front of his lady love. If she picks it up, it means yes, she will marry him. If she doesn't, the answer is no."

He set the bride back on the windowsill and reached for another nutcracker. "What does it mean when I pick up a king?" he asked.

"It means you're about to crack nuts." She slanted her head toward a bowl full of walnuts harvested the year before. "All you have to do is put the nut in the mouth and pull down on the lever."

"Sounds easier than giving your grandfather a bath," he said amicably.

⁓

After the midday meal, Lucy put her grandfather down for his afternoon nap and walked into the kitchen. She immediately noticed the tins of baked goods missing.

Puzzled, she went in search of Mr. Prescott, but he wasn't in the house. Grabbing a wrap, she let herself out the back door. It was still snowing, but not as hard as it had been. Traipsing through the knee-deep snow, she followed his footsteps to the barn. She found him attaching a canvas bag to his saddled horse.

Her heart turned over in dismay. "What are you doing?"

"Don't look so worried." He rested a hand on the

saddle. "I'm not leaving. I'm just getting ready to deliver your baked goods."

"I wasn't wor—" She cleared her throat. "You shouldn't be out in this cold. Your shoulder—"

"It's not my shoulder I'm worried about. It's my fingers and toes."

She bit her lip. "This is ridiculous. You don't even know where to make the deliveries."

He reached into his coat pocket with his left hand and pulled out the notebook containing her customer orders.

"I think I passed most of these houses looking for you."

She studied him. "Why are you being so nice to me?"

He mounted his horse and gazed down at her. "I have my reasons."

A sudden and disturbing thought occurred to her. "And would those reasons happen to have anything to do with seventy thousand dollars?"

"Seventy thousand, Miss Langdon?" His eyes gleamed. "Is that how much is in the bag you know nothing about?"

Chiding herself for her carelessness, Lucy flushed furiously. "How am I supposed to know what was in that bag?"

"Well now, I'd say that was a mighty good question." He gave her a knowing look before touching a finger to the brim of his hat. With a click of his tongue, he rode out of the barn.

Chapter 9

Lucy couldn't stay away from the parlor window for long. As much as she hated to admit it, she missed the man. She even missed his sardonic smile. But that was the least of it—she was also worried. It was snowing even harder now, and a gale force wind had started to blow.

What if he didn't come back? She discounted the possibility at once. Thanks to the slip of her tongue, he now knew for certain she had the gunnysack in her possession. Oh yes, he'd be back—of that she had no doubt.

His only concern was the money and catching those outlaws. Even he had admitted to having a one-track mind. Still, she couldn't help but wish he'd return for another reason. A more personal reason.

The thought made her grimace. Of all the dumb things that had ever crossed her mind, that had to be the dumbest. Why would a man like Mr. Prescott be interested in her? Next to his exciting life as a Texas

Ranger, he must think her dull and uninteresting.

Nor was she much to look at. She didn't have time to do herself up like some of the other single women in town. She always had flour in her hair, and oftentimes her hands were chapped and. . .

She sighed. There she went again. Feeling sorry for herself. *God forgive me.* Her duty was to take care of her grandfather and not have silly schoolgirl fantasies about a man she could never have.

∞

The next day was Christmas Eve.

Rising early, Lucy sat at the kitchen table counting the money Mr. Prescott had collected from her customers. It was enough to get the roof repaired and maybe a new pair of shoes for Opa. Her prayers had been answered.

After hiding the money in a cookie jar, she straightened the nutcracker bride on the windowsill so that it faced outward. She also said a prayer. As long as those outlaws were still on the loose, the house needed as much protection as possible.

It had stopped snowing, and a patch of blue sky stretched between the divided clouds. Pristine snow spread as far as the eye could see. The white landscape looked as stark and barren as her future.

Shaking away the depressing thought, she was just about to move from the window when a movement caught her eye. She leaned over the sink for a closer look. That's when she noticed the barn door open. Funny. She could have sworn. . .

Had Opa escaped the house?

Barely had she thought it than she spotted a man she didn't recognize walking out of the barn. Gasping, she ducked out of sight. Was that a gun in his hand?

Heart pounding, she ran to Mr. Prescott's room and without knocking, rushed inside. "Mr. Prescott." She shook him. "Wake up!"

He turned over and stared up at her. "What the—"

"Shh. There's someone outside. A stranger. He was in the barn. I think he has a gun."

Throwing the covers aside, Mr. Prescott jumped out of bed and reached for his trousers, pulling them on over his long johns. "What did he look like?"

"I don't know. I only caught a glimpse."

He quickly finished dressing, grabbed his holster on the bedpost, and raced out of the room.

Moments later the two of them were crouched in front of the parlor window. Three horses were tethered to the front fence.

"It's them," he said grimly. "The Dobson gang.

Guess we were wrong."

"Wrong about what, Mr. Prescott?"

He gave her a meaningful look. "About them taking the money out of your wagon. If the money was in their hands, they'd have no reason to come back."

He had her there. "How. . .how did they know where to find you?"

"Good question. Maybe they spotted me yesterday delivering baked goods. I should have taken your horse instead of mine. Spirit tends to stand out."

Grabbing him by the arm, Lucy dug her fingers into his flesh. "What are we going to do?" she whispered.

"Letting go of my arm would be a good start," he whispered back.

"Oh, sorry."

Something banged against the kitchen door, and Lucy jumped. A rough voice called out. "We know you're in there, Ranger."

Mr. Prescott transferred his weapon to his right hand, but he had trouble lifting his arm above his waist, so he switched back to his left.

"What kind of shot are you?" he asked.

"Accidentally or on purpose?"

"Right now I'll take it any way you can dish it out."

"In that case, I'm an excellent shot."

He nodded. "You hold down the fort while I sneak up behind them."

Cold fear knotted inside her. "That sounds like a bad idea."

"The way I see it, a bad idea is better than none." He opened a side window and checked outside. Seeing no one, he climbed over the sill. "Close it behind me," he whispered.

She slid the window shut and rushed to the kitchen for her shotgun. A sound made her whirl about. "Opa!"

Lowering her weapon, she grabbed him by the arm and led him back to the parlor.

"Eva," he muttered.

"Sit, Opa! Sit," she said in a stern voice. After settling him in his chair, she waited. The silence that followed was almost worse than the banging. She glanced out the front window. The three horses were still tethered to her fence. One by one, she checked all the windows in the house.

Just as she reached the kitchen, a gunshot rent the air. Fearful visions filled her head, and she imaged Mr. Prescott lying in the snow bleeding. *Oh God, no! Don't let anything happen to him. Please, don't!*

Holding her shotgun rigid, she moved through the kitchen, muzzle first.

Another shot, this time from a distance away. A barrage of gunfire followed. Glass shattered and sprayed over her sink.

Rising on tiptoe, Lucy chanced a quick glance outside then ducked. The three men were on her porch, backs toward her. One man was loading his gun, and the others had their weapons aimed in the direction of the barn.

The men were talking among themselves, their low voices drifting through the broken window pane. They were planning something. No time to lose. . .

Careful not to step on the broken glass, she aimed the tip of her muzzle through the shattered window. She didn't want to hurt anyone. She just wanted to chase them away.

Counting to three, she pulled back on the trigger and fired just as one of the men stood. He fell back, grabbing his arm.

"Ow, I've been hit!"

"We're surrounded," cried another.

"Let's get outta here," yelled the third, and all three fled her porch.

❧

Moments later Lucy peered through the draperies of her parlor window and watched two of the outlaws struggle to help the injured man on his horse. She waited until they had ridden out of sight before racing through the house and out the back door.

Stumbling through the snow, she called his name. "Mr. Prescott!" She was breathing hard, and her breath came out in misty white plumes. *Please God, don't let him be hurt.*

Stomach clenched, she trudged forward, her feet sinking deep into the snow.

"Mr. Prescott!" And then, "Chad!"

He stepped out from behind the barn, grinning, and her heart leaped with joy. Another prayer answered.

"Oops! You called me by my Christian name," he said. "What will your grandfather say?"

At that moment she didn't care. All that mattered was that he was alive. Closing the distance between them, she flung her arms around his neck.

"I thought you were dead," she cried.

His one good arm circled her waist, and he held her close. "Thought or hoped?"

"Don't tease," she whispered.

He gazed deep into her eyes. "If I'm dead, then this has got to be heaven," he said, his voice husky. And with that, he lowered his head and captured her lips with his own.

Chad watched Lucy traipse back to the house to check on her grandfather. He had stayed behind to calm the animals and secure the barn. He also needed to look for a piece of plywood to cover the broken window.

Lucy. Just her name made the blood pound through his veins. She was a complication he hadn't counted on. Somehow she had worked her way into his heart, and that was a problem. His job was to track down the Dobson gang, and now that he knew they were still in the area, his job got a whole lot easier.

Had his firing arm not been injured, he would have caught the scoundrels while he had the chance. No matter. He'd trailed them this far; he'd trail them to the end of the earth if necessary.

He quickly finished his tasks and headed for the house. Brrr, it was cold, and it had started snowing again. That was a blessing. He doubted the Dobson gang would make another move in this weather. Not with one being injured. That gave him a distinct advantage, but only if he acted quickly. That meant leaving the comfort of Lucy's house and getting back to work.

He paused on the porch and blew out his breath. His mouth still throbbed with the memory of her sweet lips. No matter. He had to leave, and the sooner the better, for both their sakes.

Weighed down by his thoughts, he stomped the snow off his boots and walked inside.

"Lu—"

He paused upon seeing her on the kitchen floor. She held broken pieces of wood in her hands. The bullet that shot out the window pane had shattered the nutcracker bride.

Knowing how much that particular nutcracker meant to her, he grimaced. All of this was his fault. Tossing that money into her wagon had involved her in a way he never would have imagined.

He stood the piece of plywood next to the counter and dropped to the floor by her side.

For the second time that day, he pulled her close and buried his face in her sweet-scented hair.

"What. . .what if they come back?" she whispered.

"That's why I must leave," he said. "I need to find them before they cause any more trouble."

She pulled away and looked at him. "But there're three of them, and your arm. . ."

"I won't do anything without the sheriff's help. He knows the area."

Her eyes welled with tears. "I don't want you to go."

He didn't want to go either, and that made no sense.

He wasn't one to hang around in one place for long. A week or two at the most. . .

"Staying here was a mistake. It put you and your grandfather in danger."

"You had no choice," she said. "I'm the one to blame and—"

He pressed a finger to her pretty pink lips. "It's time, Lucy."

She took his hand in hers and held it to her chest. "Today's Christmas Eve." She gave him a beseeching look. "Can't you at least stay till tomorrow?"

Common sense told him to say no, but his heart spoke louder and with more persistence.

"All right," he said. "Till tomorrow."

Chapter 10

It was snowing outside when Lucy lit the candles in the parlor that night. Her grandfather sat motionless and stared at the fire.

Chad sat whittling on a piece of wood, his trousers covered with white chips.

He'd assured her that the outlaws weren't likely to return that night, but she noticed he never strayed far from the window and was alert to every sound.

She blew out the match and tossed it into the fire. She then reached for the wooden box she'd dug out of a cupboard earlier.

"My grandfather made this crèche, and each year my grandmother set it out on the mantel," she said.

She pulled a wooden figure from its wrappings and held it up for Chad to see. It was a gray-haired shepherd in a blue robe.

Chad paused from his whittling. "Your grandfather sure did know how to dig out the best from a piece of wood."

"That he did," she said. "Each year Opa carved a new figure for the crèche and kept it secret until Christmas Eve." She smiled at the memory. "Oma and I always tried to guess in advance what he'd made, but we always got it wrong."

Altogether there were forty-six pieces. The last piece—a camel—had been made three years earlier. Never would she have guessed that it would be the last piece Opa would carve. But shortly after that Christmas, her grandfather started showing signs of forgetfulness. Soon he couldn't even remember the names of simple household items and once was unable to find his way back from the barn.

She spread a white cloth on the mantel and ran a finger across the gold stars embroidered by her grandmother. Opa'd had a fit once upon finding his initials embroidered on his long johns. "Confound it," he'd railed, "if your grandmother can't bake it, she'll embroidery it." The memory made her smile.

One by one she set each artfully crafted figure on the cloth. There were shepherds, angels, animals, and, of course, the Christ child.

She normally loved celebrating the birth of Jesus, but this year—God forgive her—sadness filled her heart. Not only would it be the first Christmas without her beloved grandmother, but tonight would be the last night spent with Chad.

She drew her strength from the Lord, but she now knew the joy of having a strong shoulder to cry on. It had only been a short while, but already she had grown accustomed to Chad's presence. She would dearly miss him.

No sooner had she put the last piece in place and stepped back to admire the holy scene than her grandfather made a funny grunting sound. He rose from his seat and headed for the door.

"Eva."

"Opa, no."

Hurrying to his side, she took hold of his arm. "It's dark and cold outside," she said gently.

"Eva!" he said again. He pulled his arm away so hard, Lucy fell back. The look on his face frightened her. Something wasn't right.

"I think the crèche upset him," Chad said.

"The cre—" Suddenly, understanding dawned. Of course. All the signs of Christmas—the crèche, the baking, the snow—reminded Opa of his wife, who loved this time of year. That's why he had been so restless of late.

Lucy reached for her grandfather's arm. This time his expression softened, and he turned away from the door of his own accord.

Only then was she aware of a soft warbling sound. Her gaze settled on Chad, who was playing what looked like a musical instrument.

Much to her surprise, her grandfather walked back to his chair unassisted.

"What is that?" she asked.

Chad pulled the wooden tube away from his mouth. "An Indian flute." He blew into the instrument again, working his fingers across the holes. "I hope you don't mind. This is the wood from the nutcracker bride."

"So that's what you've been working on." Delighted that he was able to put the broken pieces to good use, she smiled. "My grandmother loved music. It would have made her very happy to see her treasured bride turned into a musical instrument."

"Legend has it that Indians came up with the idea of making a flute after hearing the wind blow through woodpecker holes," he explained.

It was the first Lucy had ever heard of woodpeckers causing anything but problems, and she was intrigued. Mr. Holbrook often complained about the damage the birds did to his walnut trees. Just wait till she told him about the Indian flute.

She glanced at her grandfather, who looked perfectly at peace. "The music seems to calm him."

"I noticed how much he likes music," Chad said. "Thought he might enjoy some Christmas carols."

"He was fond of music, but that was a long time ago." She sighed away the memories of the past.

"He still likes music," Chad said.

Her gaze sharpened. "What makes you say that?"

"I sang while giving him a bath, and that's how I was able to get him into the water."

"You mean that awful sound—" She stopped and he laughed.

"Yep, that awful sound." The warm humor in his eyes told her he hadn't taken offense.

Chad lifted the flute to his mouth, and she recognized the tune at once as "Silent Night"—her grandmother's favorite carol—and one she called "*Stille Nacht.*"

Lucy's gaze settled on her grandfather. Something like recognition flickered in his eyes, and her heart practically burst with joy. She had almost given up hope of ever reaching him. But Chad had found a way.

She lifted her voice in song, singing first in German as Oma had often done, and then in English. She'd almost forgotten how much she enjoyed singing. Her grandmother never failed to sing while doing her chores, but Lucy had felt so overwhelmed these last few months, singing had been the last thing on her mind.

Her grandfather stayed perfectly still while she sang and Chad played. But at the song's end, a silver tear rolled down his cheek.

A cry of joy fell from Lucy's lips as she rushed to his side. It was the first real emotion he had shown in a very long time. "Don't cry, Opa." She wrapped her arms around him and held him tight and, for one glorious moment, he hugged her back.

∽

After putting Opa to bed, Lucy returned to the parlor to find Chad sitting on the floor in front of the fire, stirring the flames with the poker. She dropped to her knees by his side.

"Thank you," she whispered.

He turned his head to look at her, the flames from the fire reflected in his eyes. "For what?"

"For bringing Opa back to me." His hug had lasted only a fleeting moment, but it was something she would never forget. "You're right. Music does have a calming effect on him." For the first time in more than a week, he'd stopped trying to escape.

"Maybe music helps him feel close to his wife, and he has no need to go searching for her," Chad said.

She smiled at the thought. "Maybe you're right." She watched the dimple on his cheek fade away. "I have a present for you," she said.

"For me?"

Instead of answering him, she stood and ordered him to do the same. He replaced the poker before rising.

She turned the corner of the rug over and lifted a floorboard.

He peered down the hole. "That's not—"

"Don't look so surprised. You knew the money was here all along."

"I had my doubts," he said. "At least at first." He slanted his head and studied her. "Why now?" he asked. "Why didn't you tell me before?"

She gazed up at him and thought her heart would break. "Because I knew that the day I gave you the money was the day you would—"

Something flickered in the depths of his eyes. "Leave?"

"I didn't want you to go." She wasn't proud of what she had done, but neither could she keep lying to him.

"And now? Do you want me to go now?"

"No, but I know you must." He would not rest until he tracked down the men who killed his friend. Nor would he forgive himself for failing to do so.

"Lucy—" His hands at her waist, he gazed down at her.

She wrapped her arms around his neck. "You don't have to explain," she whispered. "But after you wear out your saddles, I hope—I pray—you'll come back."

He didn't answer her, didn't make any promises, and her heart broke into a million pieces. But even as she gazed up at him, she heard her grandmother's voice. *They call the here and now the present, Lucy, for it is a gift.*

And since the present was all that was left to them, she pushed all other thoughts aside and concentrated on memorizing every inch of his face as they talked.

And talk they did.

He told her about his sheriff father and Irish mother. About working on a Texas cattle ranch. About his friend Paul, killed in the line of duty while chasing the Dobson gang.

"He's the one who talked me into become a ranger," he said. "Between the two of us, we captured some of the worst outlaws that ever set foot in the Panhandle."

With his prompting, Lucy told him about her parents. How her grandmother instilled in her the love of literature and taught her everything she knew about cooking.

"My grandfather taught me to ride and plant crops," she said, smiling at the memory. "He also taught me how to care for animals and even showed me how to deliver a calf." It was during that time that she first became interested in anatomy. "When I told him I wanted to be a doctor, he didn't laugh. Instead, he encouraged me to work for Doc Hathaway."

Chad stared at her. "You wanted to be a doctor?"

"In the worst possible way." She smiled. "Can you imagine? A woman physician? Even the doctor was dubious, and I had to prove I was sincere. Before he would hire me, he made me stare at pictures of nudes."

Chad studied her. "Why?"

"He said I had to learn to look past the obvious so that I could concentrate on the wondrous body that God had created and learn how it worked."

"What happened? Why did you give up medicine?"

She took a deep breath. "Grandmother needed me. Taking care of Opa and running the farm and bakery was too much for her." It was too much for anyone.

"Any regrets?"

She thought about her grandfather and the tear that rolled down his cheek as he hugged her. Smiling, she shook her head. "None."

The tall case clock began to chime. "It's midnight,

Lucy," Chad whispered between kisses. "Merry Christmas."

Startled by how quickly the time had passed, Lucy reached up to smooth a wayward lock from his forehead. "Merry Christmas, Chad."

Epilogue

Spring was late that year. It was almost April, and the wildflowers were just beginning to bloom.

Lucy had worked all morning on the three-layered cake for Mary Hampton's wedding. Her grandmother had taught her how to pipe icing borders and mold flowers out of marzipan.

She forced herself to sing as she worked, though she had little heart to do so. It was only for her grandfather that she sang, as it kept him happy and content.

It was the third wedding cake she'd done that month, and each served to remind her of all she'd lost. Chad had been gone for three months, and she'd not heard a word. No letter, no telegram—nothing.

Even the sheriff had no knowledge of his whereabouts. Chad had returned the money to the bank and vanished, presumably on the trail of the Dobson gang. Was he even alive?

The possibility that he might be dead nearly crushed her, and she refused to dwell on it. She much preferred to think of him riding his black horse and wearing out his saddles.

If only she could forget his kisses. If only he didn't haunt her dreams. If only she didn't imagine seeing him, hearing him, feeling him.

She stepped back and gave the cake a critical once-over. Satisfied, she tossed the empty icing bowl into the sink and put on the kettle for tea.

A knock on the back door surprised her. Her customers usually came to the front door to pick up baked goods.

She opened the door, but no one was there. Now she was hearing things.

Moments later she heard another knock. Again, no one was there. Puzzled, her gaze traveled to the steps and her eyes widened. Something—she wasn't sure what—stood at the bottom of the porch. Something with a garish face. She walked out for a closer look and blinked.

Thinking her eyes were playing tricks on her, she ran down the steps and picked it up. This time there was no question. It was a nutcracker bride—or at least she thought it was.

The bride's gown was white and her eyes blue. Thick lashes made her look like she'd been in a fight. She had a crooked red mouth and a strange pointed chin. It was nothing like the wooden bride her grandfather gave her grandmother the day he proposed nearly half a century ago, but. . .

Puzzled, she lifted her gaze and her heart lurched. Chad stood a short distance away with a silly grin on his face. He looked even handsomer than she remembered, and much, much taller.

"Did. . .did you make this?" she asked, her voice thick with emotion.

He gave her a sheepish look and shrugged. "Not only am I a terrible singer; I'm lousy at making nutcracker brides."

She held the wooden figure to her chest. "I think it's. . .beautiful," she said, and laughed. It was the ugliest, most beautiful thing she had ever seen. She swallowed the lump that rose to her throat. "What about the Dobson gang?"

"I'm better at catching criminals. You'll be glad to know their outlaw days are over." After a beat, he added, "And so are my ranger days. I've been hired by your local county as a cattle detective. It looks like I'm gonna have to wear out my saddles chasing rustlers."

Lucy's heart leaped with joy, but she was still having a hard time believing this was real and not just another dream. "So. . .so does that mean you're staying?"

"It depends," he said.

"On w–what?" she stammered.

"On whether or not my nutcracker bride does its job."

As the meaning of his words became clear, ripples of pure happiness rushed through her. With a yelp of delight, she flew into his waiting arms.

German Zimt Makronen Cookies

(A recipe handed down from Lucy's Grandmother)

1 cup ground hazelnuts

1 teaspoon cinnamon

1 teaspoon nutmeg

1 teaspoon vanilla

4 large eggs, separated
  (need only the whites)

Pinch salt

1 teaspoon lemon juice

1 cup sugar

Whole hazelnuts to
  top cookies

Mix together ground nuts, cinnamon, and vanilla. Beat egg whites. When eggs are stiff, add lemon juice and salt. Continue to beat until stiff. Gradually fold sugar into beaten egg whites and fold in nut mixture.

Using two small spoons, place small mounds of cookie dough onto greased baking sheet. Top each cookie with a whole hazelnut and bake in a preheated oven at 350 degrees for about 20 to 25 minutes. Leave to cool. Enjoy with friends and family.

About the Author

Margaret Brownley is a bestselling author of more than thirty books. Her story was inspired by Tchaikovsky's *Nutcracker Suite* and her own collection of nutcrackers. Look for her exciting new Undercover Ladies series beginning with the release of *Petticoat Detective*, December 2014. www.margaret-brownley.com

The Gift-Wrapped Bride

by Maureen Lang

Chapter 1

Chicago, Illinois
November 1848

Boom! Snap! Pop, pop, pop!

Sophie's scream echoed the sudden whinny of horses startled by shots exploding on the busy Chicago street. Despite her grip on the wagon's seat carrying her parents, the moment the vehicle bounced off the ground, she was thrown to the narrow floorboard behind her. It was the only spot of unused space between the many belongings they'd safely toted all the way from Ohio. One of her drawing pads fell from the perch where she'd left it, a stiff corner striking her on the back of her head.

Her thirteen-year-old brother, Gordy, landed on top of her, the heel of his boot smacking her shinbone. She didn't mean to shove him away, but the wagon hit another rock or rut and she plummeted toward him, her elbow smashing into his shoulder. This time they landed side by side, just beneath the seat still miraculously holding both of her parents.

Frantic, she grappled toward the bench again, adding the new pain of a splinter to her bruises. The terror on her mother's face was plain to see, just as the sinews of her father's strong forearms stood out while he fought the reins connected to the runaway horses.

"Whoa! Dink! Acer!" The horses ignored her father's desperate call. They bounded ahead, both sets of ears pressed back, Dink's mane flying, Acer's powerful neck straining against the pull of the reins.

Suddenly from beside the wagon a new shadow joined theirs, nearly flying alongside on a road littered with other horses, wagons, even pedestrians. Anything in their path parted like a terrified Red Sea to make way for their plunge farther into town.

The shadow to Sophie's right overtook the wagon itself. It was a man on horseback, his hat flying off as he jumped from his mount and onto Dink, the strong young colt Father had been so proud to drive this far. The man leaned down just as mud spattered up in all directions. He then pulled on both horses' reins, Acer not nearly as fast as Dink but twice as strong and brave. Still, reined with Dink, he hadn't any choice except to keep up with the other horse's frenzied pace that was only now coming under control.

With the shots silenced and the added weight of a rider on his back, Dink slowed at last. Or perhaps it was the drag of mud beneath them doing the job.

"Whoa there, Dink," called her father, his voice smoother than it had been a moment ago. "Good boy, Acer. That's it. Slow him down now."

"Goodness!" said Mother, righting her bonnet, which would have flown with the wind alongside their rescuer's hat had it not been for the string tied under her chin. "What in the world caused the ruckus setting them off?"

The man on Dink glanced over his shoulder once the pair of horses came to a full stop, a stop made more secure now that they were decidedly listing to one side. Sophie felt the wagon tilt. No broken wheel or axle this time; it was a slow, rather soft slide of the wagon's entire right edge.

"Ground rats, ma'am."

"Rats! Was someone shooting at them?"

"No ma'am. Ground rats are firecrackers. They pop and sizzle and go every which way. A few landed right under your horses' hooves."

He jumped off, his own landing no doubt cushioned by the mud, but he didn't seem to mind as he patted Dink with one hand and waved a greeting to them with the other.

"Welcome to—" He stopped himself suddenly. Sophie's parents were likely the only two he'd noticed, since she was kneeling behind them and Gordy was behind her. "Mr. and Mrs. Stewart! Welcome to Chicago!"

"Look, Frank!" cried Mother. "It's Noah Jackson!"

Sophie dared another peek, her heart that still thudded from near death now pounding anew. Noah Jackson. Of all the people to greet them, why did it have to be him? That bully.

Nonetheless, she peered out, wondering if her brother Arthur might be with him. That would make the trouble that had come with their arrival worth it. But he was nowhere to be seen.

Father jumped down then moved to help Mother. Sophie watched both of them hug that wretched boy— well, she supposed he was a man now, since he certainly looked the part, with a few days of beard on his face, what she could see of it between dollops of mud. They thanked and praised him for his courage as Sophie began wondering just how convenient it was to have him play the rescuer. He'd always liked her parents, even though he treated nearly everyone else shabbily.

Perhaps he'd set off a firecracker or two just to provide himself an opportunity to show off.

Knowing she must greet him, too, especially since Gordy was already scrambling over her to get out of the wagon, she sighed heavily as Noah's face lit again with another hearty reception.

"Ha! Who's this? Not Gordy!" He slapped her little brother on the back, and to her surprise, Gordy didn't seem to mind the contact. If someone had hit her that way, she'd have called it a smack. "Maybe you're a Gordon now, little man, nearly all grown up."

"Gordy's fine. Not sure I'll answer to anything else."

Then Noah's gaze left her family as if in search of the only missing member. Her. She was still peering over the seat when he spotted her.

"Sophie?"

No sense putting it off, even though he was the last person she ever wanted to greet. Here was the boy who had single-handedly humiliated her—not just once, but on countless occasions. Tripping her in the middle of the schoolroom so her skirts went flying, petticoats and all, right up into her face for everyone to see. He was the boy who had tossed a spider onto her spelling test to make her scream. And who was punished for disrupting the class? Not him, even though she'd tattled on him. But she hadn't seen him do it and the teacher hadn't accepted her accusation against him, especially when he claimed innocence. So she'd gone alone to stand in the corner and had to stay after school to finish her test.

Noah Jackson had even put a frog in her lunch pail. She'd gone hungry that day, refusing to eat something that had no doubt been kissed by a frog.

She'd been sorry when her brother Arthur had left Toledo to come to Chicago for a job five years ago, but she hadn't been one little bit sorry when Noah announced he was going as well. Not a single member of his own large family protested his departure, although he'd been only sixteen at the time.

Clearing her throat, smoothing back her hair that had come loose from the braid barely tied at the nape of her neck, she ran a hand over her skirt, determined that both the skirt and petticoat would stay in place when she must jump off this wagon. She stood to her full height.

There was some measure of satisfaction to see Noah's eyes follow her from the height nearer what he likely remembered her to be all the way up to her current five-foot-three stature. His brows rose, and if she wasn't mistaken, she even saw a hint of appreciation in those eyes that had always been so filled with mischief.

Carefully, she climbed over the seat, choosing each movement ahead so that by the time she hopped gracefully from the step onto the only dry space nearby, she was sure he would see her for what she was. All grown up and not to be teased.

"You've grown some, Sophie," he whispered.

Mother laughed just as Father had to reach up to put a hand on Noah's shoulder.

"So have you, son."

The changes in Noah made her wonder how much Arthur had grown, too. Hadn't Mother sent him trousers on several occasions because the ones he left with had become too short?

Not wanting to give—or receive—any more attention to or from Noah, Sophie turned to see if the wagons that had been traveling behind them had caught up yet. She saw them ambling down the busy, mud-pocked road, a wave exchanged between Father and Mr. Hobson easing their neighbor's features from concerned to his usual placid face.

In the same sweep, Sophie also took in the sights of the street. It was just as cluttered as it had been before clearing the way for their wild ride, but Arthur was nowhere to be seen along the string of shops.

Although this street offered mostly wooden store-fronts and uneven boardwalks, she had to admit this town was larger than Toledo. Not that it was better—she smelled the unmistakable odor of livestock—but at least they wouldn't have to live in that wagon anymore. The past four weeks of that had been enough.

"Isn't Arthur with you?"

Sophie was glad her mother had asked what she'd wanted to, and looked again at Noah for his answer. She was surprised to see he'd still been looking at her but snapped his gaze to her mother when he caught her observation.

"He must be done at the Reaper Works for the day but likely went straight to look for you once the whistle blew."

"He got the job there then?" asked Father.

Noah nodded. "Now that the canal is finished, a bunch of us were glad to get good jobs elsewhere, sir. I'm working with the Mechanics group myself."

Sir. Humph. Noah Jackson hadn't changed a bit. He had always sounded respectful around her father. Why didn't Noah talk to him the way he used to talk to everyone else? Clever name calling was Noah Jackson's specialty. "Squealer Sophie" had been a favorite, not to mention "String Bean Sophie" because of her skinny arms, and "Swan Sophie" because he said her neck was too long. Most of the time he'd called her "Tot," short for toddler, which sufficiently reminded her she was four years younger than Arthur. As if that would make Noah more than just two years older than her.

"Arthur wrote to us about the place to camp our wagons, Noah," Father said. "Do you know where it is?"

"Up on the Des Plaines Valley Road. I'll take you there. The site's about a half hour or so north."

"So far?" Gordy complained. "I thought we were here already. In our new home."

"And so you are," Noah said, tousling Gordy's light brown hair. "It's a spot for wagon trains going west to assemble while they purchase everything they'll need. Plenty of room for those coming to town, too, to settle in until everybody figures out where to live."

Father waved again to Mr. Hobson, who had pulled up behind them. "Noah Jackson's here," he called, "and he'll take us to a place to camp."

Mr. Hobson saluted his acknowledgment, and Sophie spotted the head of her friend Alice pop up behind him. As much as Sophie loved her best friend, she had to hide the scowl she'd just inspired. Alice was likely looking for a peek at one of the "young prospects," the main and awful reason she and Sophie and several other daughters had been dragged to Chicago in the first place. But really, did Alice want a peek at the bottom of the barrel?

Sophie meant to have a serious talk with that girl.

Noah moved back toward the horses. "We'll get you out of this mud hole first."

Sophie moved out of the way. Perhaps she would ride with Alice and start that talk right now. "I've never been so grateful for mud," she grumbled as she pulled her skirts clear of another puddle between her and the nearest wooden walkway.

Mother sent her a surprised look, Father a frown, and Noah a quizzical stare. In spite of the attention, she had no wish to call back her words. "It's what stopped us, wasn't it? The mud?"

Noah raised one of his brows but said nothing, as her mother tsked.

"That's a little like thanking the fire for a hot meal, dear. We wouldn't have anything to eat without the cook."

"What do you mean, Mother?" Gordy asked.

Sophie tilted her head, staring at her mother even though she felt Noah's gaze more strongly than any other. "She means Noah's the cook."

"Oh! Sure, that's right." Gordy's face burst into a

smile. "I get it now. 'Cause it was him who saved us. Not the mud. Right, Mother?"

Sophie couldn't help but roll her eyes as she tugged her little brother along. Father went to Acer's side while Noah went around to Dink's, and between the two of them they coaxed the animals to pull the rig free of the soft, stubborn earth.

Sophie folded her arms. Noah Jackson might have grown into a strong, even handsome young man. She couldn't help but notice the way his shoulders strained the material on that gray cotton shirt he wore. He had the same bold brows, broad chin, and thick, dark hair— hair that reached past the folded collar of his shirt.

But he was no hero. She knew that as sure as she knew Chicago was the last place on earth she wanted to live.

Chapter 2

For the first time in five years, Noah Jackson was living in better conditions than the folks he and Arthur had left behind in Ohio. The boardinghouse he called home since they'd finished living in tent quarters along the canal construction wasn't much better—it was more like a dormitory above the long, wide stable below—but it had a solid roof, rope beds with straw mattresses, and real windows. All of that made it far better than sleeping under a cramped wagon or the crowded four-room home he grew up in with seven brothers and sisters.

It wouldn't be long before he and Artie introduced Artie's folks to all the possibilities that Chicago offered. Soon they'd be settled in a proper home.

Pulling on his boots, he called to Arthur, still sleeping on the cot next to his own.

"Hey, better get going, Artie. Church in a half hour."

"Huh?"

"Half hour. Let's go."

Arthur Stewart had only one thing in common with his sister: they shared the same color hair. Noah would never have bothered to describe the shade—a mix of gold and copper—until seeing it on Sophie. He wondered if he'd ever be able to look at Arthur again without thinking of her.

Which was too bad for him. She'd made a point to ignore him all the way to the campsite and forever thereafter.

Sophie had been mighty happy to see her brother though. She'd laughed, because even though Artie was taller than she was, her brother's height had stopped at the same spot as their father. She'd teased Gordy, saying that was likely all the taller he'd get, too.

Had she noticed how tall Noah had gotten? But then, how would she, when she made such a point to ignore him?

Who would have thought that little tattler would grow into such a lovely young woman? He knew she'd matured, because Artie had shared her letters with him over the years. Letters that hadn't failed to impress, even intrigue Noah—something he'd kept to himself.

As usual, Artie was slow in the morning, even on Sunday after an extra hour of sleep. When they'd come to Chicago that was how Noah had been, too, especially on Sunday, a day both had proclaimed a day of rest, even from something like church.

But that had all changed once they'd met Ezra Pooley, the canal foreman's father. Ezra was a patriarch of Chicago who had the goodwill—some might call it bad sense—to invite young men far from their homes into his own. Tasty meals, interesting conversations, even the patience to teach whoever cared to learn the craft of leather working. He'd given Noah plenty to think about, including God.

Ezra had also helped the boys investigate land and housing available if their families did decide to come to Chicago. Noah was sure their findings had encouraged his friends' families to leave Toledo for the promise of such a growing city like Chicago.

"Better wear that tie," Noah reminded Artie, who was still sitting on the side of his cot, rubbing palms to his face against remnants of sleep.

A light of anticipation ignited on Arthur's face. "Oh yeah! We didn't take baths for nothin' last night, did we? We can reacquaint ourselves with the girls today. My parents said so themselves."

"Hush up!" called a voice a few bunks away. "Some of us are trying to sleep."

"And we're no louder than O'Hananan's snoring,"

Noah said back, "so hush up yourself." He pulled the duffel bag from beneath his cot, taking up his comb and facing Artie again. "I counted four, besides your sister, of course," he whispered. "That's five. Did I miss any?"

"Ha! Shows you how much you saw past Sophie. I saw you watching her. There are eight. Two in the Hobson family, three in the Cabots', one each in the Hatten and the Selway wagons."

"Two in the Hobson family? Alice is one. But you're not counting Sally, are you? She can't be any older than twelve."

"She's fifteen, and in a couple of years she'll be just as pretty as her sister."

"I'm surprised you saw anybody past Alice then, if you think I didn't see anybody but Sophie."

"It was Sophie who told me how many came along. I think the pastor brought his sister, too, but Sophie didn't count her, because she's old enough to have stayed behind." Then he cleared his throat, as if buying time to figure out what to say next. "Uh, there's something I should say about Sophie. She's not too keen on why my family decided to join us out here. Says they're putting all their daughters up on the marriage block like 'common property.'"

Noah laughed at Artie's imitation of Sophie. He'd done a good job at capturing her disdain.

"If only it were that easy," he said with an exaggerated sigh. "Just to hand over some of our savings and buy one."

Artie took a friendly swipe at Noah with the tie he would wear over one of the two new shirts his mother had brought with them—Noah was wearing the other. "Hey, that's my sister you're wanting to buy as if she's on Chicago's cattle market. A little bit of wooing will do both of you some good."

"A little bit of wooing?" Noah repeated. "You think that's all it'll take?"

Artie laughed all the way to the door.

⌘

Sophie let Alice loop their arms, but it wasn't a solely affectionate gesture. Her friend surely knew that if Sophie wasn't coerced into going to this afternoon's meeting, she wasn't likely to attend at all. Why Alice and Martha and Jane and even little Sally and the rest of those who'd been brought from Ohio wanted to be here was beyond Sophie's understanding. She'd much rather stay back at the detestable wagon. At least there she could pass the time drawing the birds she'd seen on the trail here—something she hadn't been able to do during the entire bumpy ride west. She only hoped she could remember the details she'd tried committing to memory along the way.

She'd had to ignore the stares of several young men at this morning's church service behind the wagons. Not the least of which was Noah Jackson's. Word had evidently spread that five foolish families from the East had come to town ready to add themselves to the Chicago census, both now and in the future, by bringing a crop of potential new brides.

Many men of Chicago were responding, even if the first price to pay had been sitting through a church service. The pastor had welcomed his new congregation while silly girls like Alice beamed under the attention. Sophie wished she could have crawled under Father's bench, away from the obvious scrutiny.

This afternoon's meeting was supposed to address how best to proceed with their resettlement as well as the procurement of a new church building. She'd heard her father and mother discuss such things all the way from Ohio, as if jobs and homes and the church were their only concerns.

But the real reason for coming to Chicago was the one topic they carefully avoided around Sophie. It was, in fact, the true incentive behind today's meeting. Now, boys like Noah Jackson, Alice's brother Howard, the Selway and Hatten boys—all who had come to Chicago for jobs—would be allowed to look over their sisters and neighbors and see just how mature they had become.

Wife material.

"You changed your clothes from the service this morning," Alice said as they approached the gathering spot behind their row of wagons. Tables had been added to the benches and chairs they'd used for the service, so it now looked like the setting for a party.

"I'm more comfortable now."

"And why have you pinned up your hair that way?" The disapproval in her friend's tone was clearer now. "It looks better free and down your back. Or maybe a single braid tied loosely like you did yesterday—a little softer than what you have."

Sophie was half tempted to unfasten the tight bun at the back of her head, but not for the reason Alice suggested. She'd pulled it so severely away from her face it was giving her a headache. However, that, combined with her oldest and most faded skirt and topped by a thick and unnecessary shawl on this uncommonly lovely fall day, were her only methods of protest. She wasn't here to exhibit herself.

"I can't understand why you're willing to go along with this scheme to throw us together with the boys already here," Sophie said. "It's not natural."

"Oh fiddle-faddle. What's unnatural about providing an opportunity to fall in love and start a new life? No one's forcing us to get married, you know. I think we should be grateful to be here, where brides are needed far more than they are back in Toledo. We'll have more choice here."

Back in Toledo. . . Chicago might be bigger, but Sophie had left behind the one dream that was more important to her than marriage. Mr. Allenby was like a grandfather to her. After taking her under his wing three years ago, he'd taught her more about wildlife drawing than she could ever have learned on her own. He'd assured her that her drawings were good enough to be appreciated by anyone who saw them, often telling her of his friend in New York who published such pictures in books. Real books that might have someday included her own drawings.

Each and every thought of leaving such a future behind came with a pinprick of pain. She couldn't see a bird fly or a mouse scurry across the plains without wondering what could have happened had Mr. Allenby introduced her drawings to his friend, as he'd promised to do when next he had the opportunity.

With a sigh, Sophie looked around. Others were already assembled with her parents and Alice's parents. Although Alice pulled her forward, Sophie held back, lingering near the third table. They were close enough to catch her mother's eye, however, and she gave Sophie a surprised glance at the skirt she'd worn through most of their travels. Her mother's frown sent a silent question Sophie could nonetheless hear loud and clear: *Why don't you just cover yourself in sackcloth and ashes?*

Sophie looked past her mother to a new source of resentment. The pastor's wife and three other women, all mothers, tended to the bowls and trays set off on a table to the side. On any other occasion, girls like herself and Alice would be serving the older folks. But no, not today. They didn't want the girls distracted with work when there were gazes to catch, smiles to exchange. Love to inspire.

"You're looking especially pretty this afternoon," came a familiar voice behind them.

Sophie and Alice turned around. It was Arthur, looking directly at Alice. As she giggled and thanked him for the compliment, Sophie felt like teasing him about playing Romeo. But when she saw Noah Jackson at his side, the temptation to add anything lighthearted to the afternoon abandoned her.

Arthur's eyes settled next on Sophie, where he started to smile anew but then looked outright confused. "And you, Sophie, well, you look pretty awful. That hair looks to be wound tighter than when I used to yank it. Why don't you let it go?"

"Because I like it this way." She turned around at the table, offering them her back as she took a seat and tugged on Alice to do the same. Unfortunately, rather than moving on, the boys claimed places just opposite. Arthur sat across from Alice, and Noah across from Sophie.

"It sure is nice to see some familiar faces around here," Noah said, briefly glancing at Alice but letting his gaze rest on Sophie. "I forgot how good it is to be around somebody I've known my whole life, other than just Artie."

Sophie raised her nose and looked away. "Then I suppose you know how hard it was for Alice and me to leave behind friends we've had all our lives, too."

"Aw, Sophie," said Arthur, "you brought along half the ones you know best. You weren't closer to anybody than Alice. Can't complain too much about that."

Shows you how much you know, she wanted to say. Hadn't he read any of her letters? She'd even sent him some of her favorite drawings, to show him how much Mr. Allenby had taught her. Her brother had obviously forgotten all about that. From the look on his face when he ogled Alice, she could see why.

But then he glanced back at her. "I suppose you miss Mr. Allenby. Guess I don't blame you for that."

Sophie was so surprised he'd spoken her thoughts that she wouldn't trust her voice not to reveal the depth of her loss. Alice quickly filled the growing pause.

"She certainly does miss that old man," Alice said. "Not that he wasn't kind, and a talented artist and teacher, too. But I keep telling her he was, well"—she tapped her temple—"addled. Do you know he used to call me by my mother's name? And his neighbor saw him in his bathrobe on his front stair! He said he was looking for his hat. Outside!"

"He's an artist," Sophie reminded Alice. "Artists are always flamboyant."

"I'm sorry you miss him," Noah said softly, his gaze still on her. "Arthur and I have met that kind of man here, the kind to share his time. He's taught me leather working. Guess I'd miss him if we left town."

Sophie spared him a glance, but not for long. She was waiting for him to come up with a new nickname for her. If she were to think of one for herself with her hair fashioned the way she'd pulled it back today, it would be "Tufted Duck." If she drew a picture of one now, he would think of the name himself.

"And did he teach you how to make ground rats, perhaps?" She hadn't meant to say that aloud, and when all eyes turned to her, she almost wished she could recall them. Almost.

"Father told me about how Noah saved the rig," Arthur said. "You don't really think Noah set off that ruckus so he could risk his life trying to stop it?"

She didn't reply, letting her silence speak for her.

"That is what you believe then?" Noah persisted. She was surprised to hear a touch of sadness in his voice.

It was that very sadness that angered her now, just as much as the defense her brother had launched for him a moment ago. "Why shouldn't I assume such a thing? You, who tripped me whenever you had the chance, embarrassing me in front of the entire classroom? You, who waited behind bushes until I was in range of your slingshot to shoot peas at me? You, who started that fire in the school outhouse? You, who made sure I was startled out of my wits right over a puddle and made me drop my books into it. And those are only a few of my memories of you, Noah Jackson. Why wouldn't you do something like set off a few firecrackers?"

He whistled low. "You have a better memory than I do. And here I thought you were just Tot the Tattler. Guess you had some reasons for it though."

Such a feeble attempt to claim responsibility was hardly enough to excuse his behavior. He might have been gone five years, but she doubted that was long enough to have changed him. That would take eternity.

"Sophie," Arthur said, his tone exasperated, "Noah didn't pull such a childish—and dangerous—prank like setting off firecrackers under a horse in the middle of a busy street. That happens more than you'd imagine, with or without Noah around. Fact is, there's a group of boys in town that like creating mischief." He looked around, his gaze stopping in the direction of their parents. "In fact, I was going to warn Father to keep Gordy clear of them. Where is Gordy anyway?"

Sophie threw a glance back toward their wagon but didn't see their brother. "He was going to stay in the wagon during the meeting—until the food is ready, of course."

"We'll talk to him directly then," Noah said, "after we eat."

Just then the pastor called their attention to say the blessing. Before bowing her head, Sophie stole a quick look at Noah. He appeared downright pious as he prepared to join in prayer, but she didn't believe his act for a moment.

A pious bully? Huh!

Chapter 3

In the next two weeks, Sophie learned just how valuable it had been for the families coming west to have had their sons pave the way. In anticipation of their arrival, Arthur had not only helped explore housing possibilities, but jobs and schools and the best furniture makers in town. Father was a factory millwright with experience, so his talents were in demand anywhere a factory with machinery could be found. In spite of workers already available in the city left without a job once canal work was finished, good references and the associations offered through their sons had each father a job by the end of the very first week.

Even Sophie had to admit it was only Mr. Allenby she missed, because the home Arthur had found for them in Chicago was every bit as comfortable, plus a little larger, than the one they had left behind. And she still had the company of her best friend.

At the family dinner table one evening, Noah assured her family that Chicago would far surpass Toledo.

Of course he would think so. Hadn't he helped Arthur convince their family to move here? She refused even to listen to him, leaning closer to Arthur to ask him a question she'd had nearly since their arrival.

"Is there a library here in town?"

"Several."

Sophie looked at Noah, who had usurped the answer before her brother could speak. Try though she did to avoid speaking to Noah, he seemed to have a response to everything she said, even when not directed to him.

"The libraries here in Chicago are connected to private clubs," Arthur added. "Women aren't allowed membership."

"Not at Gale and Company," Noah said. He looked at Sophie, but she averted her face even though she hung on his words. "It's a store, but they have a small circulating library, too. I can take you there tomorrow afternoon."

"I'm sure I can find it on my own," she said.

"If they don't have the kind of book you're looking for, I can introduce you to Mr. Pooley. He has quite a few books that I'm sure would interest you."

"Thank you, but I'm sure that won't be necessary." She turned her attention back to her dinner, ignoring the slight tap on her ankle from her mother.

Sophie didn't even look at Mother. She knew she would send a reminder of the gentle advice she'd offered earlier. Be pleasant, be friendly, smile at the boy. He's only trying to be nice.

Sophie had no intention of adhering to any of it. Her mother was too easily fooled by the thin veneer over Noah's bullying ways. Gullibility around someone like Noah could be downright hazardous.

∞

"What a pleasant surprise!"

Sophie looked up from the book on the small table in front of her but offered no greeting as Noah took the empty seat on the other side. Wasn't sharing most of her family's dinners with him enough? Now he had to follow her to the library, too?

"Did you know I'm working with the Chicago Mechanics' Institute? I stop in here often because this is on my way home."

So that was the reason he'd been so eager to tell her about the library.

"It has mostly fiction, but it's a nice variety." She kept her voice polite but curt then looked again at the book before her. He did not take the hint to leave her to it. "I'm sure you'll want to be on your way then. Good day."

He remained seated comfortably. There was only one way to end this, and that was to see about borrowing this book even though she wasn't at all sure this was the one she wanted. Exploring others would have to wait until next time.

Pulling the book closer to her side of the table, she stood. Noah jumped to his feet as well.

"In a hurry?"

"Yes," she said, but was instantly convicted of her lie. "No. I simply want to speak to the clerk."

"Don't forget about the private collection I mentioned," he said. "Ezra Pooley's. Arthur knows him, too. I visited him just the other day, and I noticed he has a book you might like. A bound copy of Wilson's *American Ornithology*. Have you ever seen it, Sophie?"

Her pulse quickened. "Not a bound copy," she admitted. Mr. Allenby owned several loose plates, but not the entire collection. What a treasure such a book would be! Even just to look at. . .

Her heart missed a beat at the opportunity, but she turned away. "Then I'll ask Arthur about him. Good day."

"Sophie," he called softly after her when she took a few steps away, "are you ever going to forgive me for a few childish pranks?"

She faced him head on. "All I've seen since we arrived is the way you used to act around my parents. Very polite, but I'm afraid not very sincere. So I'm sure you'll understand if I repeat myself. Good day."

"No, wait, Sophie." He touched her elbow lightly to prevent her from moving on again. "Even if you don't think I've changed, you must admit I've grown up. Hasn't Arthur told you that?"

"My entire family has been on a veritable campaign for you. But frankly, even if I believed a word of it, I have no intention of forgetting that you have the heart of a bully. Now really, *good day*."

Her heart pounded harder than the heels of her boots on the wooden floor. If she'd been rude, she'd given him no less than what he deserved.

Why should she believe he'd changed? She knew how busy Arthur and Noah had been these last few years, between working on the Illinois and Michigan Canal and whatever jobs they could find when canal work had been interrupted. Such labor might have made them both stronger, but work hadn't been the only thing they'd done since they left Toledo.

She'd read every letter Arthur had sent, and couldn't help hearing Noah's since her mother read aloud those he'd sent to her parents. For the first four and a half years, all they'd talked about was one pub or another, often places where fights broke out. They'd lived the lives of wild young men without church or civility. Exactly how was Noah to have improved himself in a place like this?

Holding the book more gently now that she was away from him, she ventured a glance behind her, but he was already gone. Assuring herself her own rudeness couldn't possibly penetrate such a thick hide as his, she walked on. Likely he'd already forgotten their encounter.

∞

Noah waited just outside Gale and Company. For two weeks, ever since Sophie had made it clear she remembered every foolish thing he'd ever done, he'd kept himself busier than ever. When he wasn't occupied, he tried thinking about some of the other girls who had come to Chicago with their families.

But it was no use. Even if Noah were interested, competition for polite female company was stiff in this city. If he encouraged a fledgling interest in any of them, there was already a long line of beaus waiting for her. He had little desire to fight for anyone's attention except Sophie's.

The only reason he did not have to wade through a

long line at Sophie's door was because she didn't seem any friendlier toward the others than she was toward him. Arthur told him when a caller came to introduce himself to Sophie, she asked her mother to send him away without seeing him.

Still, it was only a matter of time before her attitude was bound to soften about having left Toledo. Noah planned to use his close proximity to the family to his benefit around the one girl whose interest he genuinely wanted to stir.

"Fight! Fight!"

The call came from across the street, where passers-by were already circling a couple of young boys locked in a scuffle. No one seemed interested in doing anything more than watch, even when one broke free long enough to land a punch against the other boy's cheek.

"Hey!" Noah jumped through the crowd, knowing all too well that a fight lasting only a few minutes could feel like it went on forever. Not to mention leave more than a little sting. He grabbed the larger of the two boys—who was still a foot shorter than Noah himself—while he staved off the other with the long length of his arm. Working on the pumps regulating the water level along the canal had made Noah stronger than ever.

"Punching each other isn't going to stop whatever gripe you have," he said. "You'd better not fight on the street, or you'll both get fined for public nuisance. Now go home and work out some other way to settle this."

He shoved off both of them. His intervention was likely nothing more than a delay to yet another fight, but at least they wouldn't be doing it with an audience of women and children. At least he hoped not.

He would have returned to the bookshop to wait for Sophie, but one of the other spectators caught his glance. This boy hadn't run off as fast as the rest of the gang of rogues.

"Gordy?"

The boy stopped, his back still to Noah. It took ten steps to reach him, and with each one Noah held out hope he was wrong. But he wasn't.

"I hope you just happened by," Noah said, but Gordy's guilty face told him otherwise. "You haven't been mixing with that group of boys, have you, Gordy? In spite of what Artie and I told you?"

Gordy plunged his hands into the pockets of his knee pants, hanging his head so all Noah could see was the top of his cap.

"They're friendly. To me."

"You don't think sooner or later you'll get in a fight

with one of them, or do something you shouldn't be doing?"

Gordy squared his shoulders. "I know better than that. But a fella's got to have friends. Friends my own age."

"Gordy!"

Sophie's call came from the sidewalk on the other side of the street.

Gordy's eyes sprang to his sister then back to Noah, for the first time with a hint of fear in them.

"You aren't going to tell her, are you, Noah?"

Noah needed more than a few scant seconds to answer such a question, and Sophie joined them before he'd come close to any decision.

"Didn't you go straight home from school today, Gordy?" asked Sophie.

Gordy shook his head, even though his gaze hadn't yet left Noah's. Under any other circumstance, Noah would have had no intention of tattling, at least for now. But he was treading carefully around Sophie and wondered if withholding something she'd likely find important would sit well if she ever found out.

"I'll escort both of you home," Noah announced, and to his surprise Sophie didn't object. But she did walk in front of him, taking Gordy by the arm in just the way he hoped she would take his someday. Easily, as if it were the most natural thing in the world.

"You staying for dinner, Noah?" Gordy threw the tentative question over his shoulder.

Noah knew his answer wouldn't meet the boy's full approval, as it might have only an hour ago—before learning a good talking-to was in store.

The very same answer was likely received by Sophie with the same lack of welcome—he couldn't see her face—but he offered a broad and confident smile anyway. "Sure am!"

Chapter 4

Sophie heard only two sounds: a faint rustle from the tall, browned grass on the prairie in the distance, and the scratch of the pencil against her notepad. She'd had to walk some distance to get here this morning, but the sky was clear and a southern breeze comfortably warmed the air. She'd been eager to leave behind the noise and smells along the busy streets and so had left just after dawn lit her way.

Mr. Allenby once told her real wildlife artists would use specimens from taxidermists whenever they could, or on their own might wire a small, dead animal in place to allow thorough study for recording each detail with minute precision. Other than the time Alice's cat had delivered a dead bird to her, which her friend promptly offered to Sophie, Sophie had neither the wherewithal to kill nor the desire to carry through with such measures, even in the name of art or science.

Back in Toledo she would often do what she did now. Sit quietly and study whatever God sent her way.

She had to depend on her own observational skills, since most animals did not stay long to pose. But her initial drawings were always swift, and her memory was strong. She kept her drawings in her notebook, and whenever she saw a bird she'd already documented, she would check again to be sure she'd recorded it as accurately as a live bird would allow.

With her mind as quiet as her surroundings, Sophie realized she'd accepted sooner than she expected this move away from Toledo. The prairie was lovely with its tall, swaying grasses. It would provide all kinds of new animals to draw, she was sure of it. She certainly missed Mr. Allenby—he was a good teacher, after all. But perhaps what she really missed was his promise to introduce her work to an important publisher.

It still pained her to recall what Father had said when she'd protested leaving behind her opportunities and artistic aspirations. He'd claimed Mr. Allenby was nothing more than a friendly, harmless old man with no real idea how to get her drawings published. As fine as her drawings might be, there were plenty of others who would see their work published long before hers ever would be.

She knew he hadn't meant to be cruel; in his way, he might even have been trying to protect her from hoping for something he thought impossible. But as she reviewed the drawing she'd just finished, of a bird she couldn't name, with a stark red streak fringed with a contrasting white along the top of its black wings, she knew her work was true to life. It was good enough to be published. *Wasn't it?*

"Sophie! Sophie!"

Sophie stiffened at the call of her name coming from two different directions. There was no hill or canyon to make an echo. Who could be calling for her out here?

She stood.

"I'm here!"

She saw her brother first from one direction then Noah from another, both trotting closer, and each out of breath, with considerable concern on their faces.

"What's the matter?" she demanded. "Is everyone all right? Mother? Father? Not trouble with Gordy?"

Arthur exchanged a curious look with Noah before they both burst into laughter. "Everybody's worried about *you*, you great big ninnyhammer," he said, gently shoving her shoulder.

"Why in the world would anybody worry about me? I told Mother where I was going."

"Yes, and she told Father, who told me when I came

by for breakfast. I started the alarm. I fetched Noah immediately and wouldn't let Gordy or even Father come along for fear of losing either one of them."

Clutching the notepad closer to her chest, Sophie cast a glance at Noah, who was still looking on with an annoyingly clear residue of concern. "I have no idea why you should have sounded such an alarm."

"The prairie's a dangerous place, Sophie," Noah said softly. "Even here, close to the city. It's easy to get lost in the tall grasses, for one, not to mention the snakes and wolves."

Lifting her chin, Sophie started back home exactly the way she'd come. "Despite what you might think, I'm not a *complete* ninnyhammer." She kept walking without looking back. "I'd know enough not to get myself lost, and as for wolves and snakes, the grasses are still a ways off, so there wasn't much risk of that either."

Although she never looked back at either one of them, she felt their presence as clearly as if they'd been breathing down her neck.

"What's that you're holding there, Sophie?" called Noah.

She pretended not to hear him.

"That's her drawing book," her brother answered. "Don't you remember? I showed you some of the pictures she sent in letters."

"Oh sure," Noah said. "You're pretty good, Sophie. So what did you draw today?"

Pretty good. He obviously shared the same tendency for meager praise her father possessed, at least when it came to her talent. What other words went with *pretty good*? *Tolerable, passable, satisfactory.* Each of those terms would hardly inspire an artist to greater effort.

Unless. . .that was all the regard her talent deserved.

She increased her pace, not speaking a word all the way back to the house, where Mother offered everyone a delayed breakfast.

Sophie went straight to her room and didn't emerge again until after Father, Arthur, and Noah left for their jobs.

∞

"So you think they're pretty good then?"

Noah felt little compunction about having borrowed Sophie's drawings from Arthur's letters even though he hadn't asked him. He watched Ezra Pooley's lined face for any sign that he could be wrong, that his infatuation with Sophie had fooled him into thinking her drawings were good enough to interest others besides himself and Arthur, both of whom shared definite partiality toward the artist. Ezra was as honest as he was old, and Noah knew he could depend on him for an unbiased opinion.

When Ezra raised his brows, Noah knew he was right. Sophie's talent was every bit as real as he believed it to be.

"They're very good." Ezra stroked his chin. "And you think readers will be interested in these pictures?"

Ezra's opinion had already emboldened Noah. "Don't you? There's nothing more popular than the pictures of the West in the *Democrat*. Why not give people the same visual gift about their own backyard? Newcomers and others just passing through will be interested in knowing what to look for around here, or on the prairie if they make plans to move on."

"Illustrations increase the cost," Ezra said, but added a grin before Noah's hopes could be dashed. "And there won't be any colors. But I think your idea is sound, and I can suggest a name or two at the papers who can afford such a thing—starting with the *Prairie Farmer*."

Chapter 5

"And so, dear brethren, let our hearts stay warm toward the God who watches over us and sees our every action. Let us plan the remembrance of Christ's birth with love in our hearts for those outside the church, because we may be the only glimpse of God's love others will see. Amen and amen."

Sophie filed out of the pew behind her family. Everyone was jubilant over the new building Pastor Goodwin had found in the city, even though the facts behind its availability might be something they would prefer not to think about. Another church had tried establishing itself, only to fail, leaving their quarters vacant. Didn't anyone worry such a cycle might repeat itself in this muddy, stinking city?

Outside, Sophie turned up her collar against the wind. At least with colder temperatures the mud had hardened, but that was small comfort against the biting gusts.

She drew her brows together as she watched Gordy,

walking ahead of them toward home, three blocks from church. Earlier in the week, he had been the cause of one of their mother's rare sour moods, but with good reason. While she and Sophie were baking bread, Gordy's teacher paid them a visit. Her brother had taken to coming home late after school, saying he was spending time with friends. But his teacher informed them he hadn't come to school at all that day.

Sophie couldn't help but wonder if Gordy wasn't taking after Noah, despite the lack of a blood tie.

"You'll help me with the costuming, won't you, dear?"

Sophie was startled when her mother put an arm about her shoulder, shaking her from her thoughts. They walked on arm-in-arm, and she was grateful to share her mother's warmth.

"What's that, Mother?"

"For the nativity pageant. Haven't you been listening? The pastor mentioned he hopes the Christmas season will draw people to church." She sighed, her gaze on Gordy, too. "I'm hoping the fun of a pageant will keep Gordy busy with better things to do than spend time with boys who don't think school is important."

"Yes, I'll help—if I'm needed, that is. I don't think Pastor Goodwin has had much success recruiting participants." She didn't bother to veil the glare she sent her mother's way. "Those of us who came from Toledo were more concerned about bringing brides, Mother. There is only one Mary in the nativity. Evidently we should have brought more boys than just Gordy."

Instead of being offended at Sophie's reminder of why they'd come to Chicago, Mother laughed and patted her shoulder. "All we want is to provide a happy life for our children, dear. As the saying goes, a shared life is twice as pleasant and half as hard. Jane Cabot is ready to prove that already."

Sophie grimaced. Jane was the first of the girls they'd traveled with to become engaged, and everyone was talking about their New Year's wedding. The silly way Alice and Arthur were acting, she guessed they might be next to announce upcoming nuptials.

The prospect of watching the girls go down one by one, like ducks at a hunt, seemed abjectly unjust. So obviously contrived. And yet, somehow, the thought of being the only one not to marry presented an unexpected worry.

What else was she to do but marry if she couldn't follow her dream of drawing wildlife?

∾

Noah grabbed the collar of the boy he recognized as having been one of the participants in the fight he'd witnessed not long ago. Holding him at arm's length, he ignored the boy's protests over having been waylaid on the boardwalk on South Water Street.

"I have a proposition for you and your friends," Noah said over the boy's shout.

"I don't want no proposition! Lemme go!"

"How do you know you don't want something you haven't even heard yet?"

Noah let go of the frayed collar, only to grab hold of the boy's shoulders. With the temperature growing so much colder, it was a wonder the boy had left whatever home he had with such thin protection—if he even had a home.

"What's your name, boy?"

"None o' your business."

"That's where you're wrong. I live in this town, and you're a troublemaker for all of us. So you made it my business."

"You're dotty! Now lemme go!"

He attempted to break free, but Noah's height and strength had the advantage. It occurred to him the boy had a right to his own freedom, and if anyone saw the exchange he'd likely find himself—not the boy—in trouble. But he wasn't ready to give up on his idea so easily.

"Look," said Noah, "I know you must be one of the most loyal members of your pack or else you wouldn't have had the grit to fight. You'd have let somebody else do the fighting. I want to talk to you and the rest of the boys you haunt with."

The boy's struggle eased just enough to let Noah think he wouldn't run off if given the chance. So he let go. The boy shrugged at his jacket, setting it right on his shoulders again. But he stayed put, although the suspicion on his face wasn't any friendlier than the anger had been a moment ago.

"Whata ya wanna talk about?"

"I have a job for you. It's only for a season, but worthwhile. It could lead to other opportunities." *And it might be the only way to keep an eye on Gordy.*

The boy huffed. "Sure. You got a job for a bunch o' boys when this town's filled with grown Irishmen who can't get a job since canal work got done."

"It's a job only young people can do."

"What kind o' job?"

Noah regarded the boy curiously. "Maybe you'd better let me talk to your friends. I'd rather give everybody the chance to answer without you making up their minds ahead of time."

The boy seemed to take it for what it was, a

compliment on the power of a leader's influence. "Meet us back o' the tavern down the street in an hour," he said. "The Hog's Head."

Noah would have thanked him for the name, since so many streets in the city hosted more than one tavern. But the boy ran off. Noah called after him. "Hey, kid, what's your name?"

"Still none o' your business."

Then he was gone.

∞

"You call that a job?" Tully repeated.

The only reason Noah had learned the boy's name was because he'd heard someone else address him. He knew this was taking a chance, a "dotty" one as Tully might say, but there was bound to be a boy or two who could be convinced to join the nativity pageant in exchange for what he had in mind.

"What's a job except an exchange of goods and services?" Noah scanned the patched clothing—near rags—some of the boys wore. "You get a meal at every practice—one you won't have to steal. You get a warm place to eat it, and at the end you get a coat to see you through till spring."

"All for dressing up like loons?"

"Shepherd boys." He looked around. "And three will get to be kings."

There was a titter here and there, a general consensus as to who should play one of the kings, but Tully stopped their rumblings with a shout. "Hey! This ain't no kingdom, so you can all make up your own minds. I think it's pure twaddle. Anybody who does it'll make a fool of hisself."

Another boy, the one Noah recognized as having been on the other end of the fight he'd broken up, stepped closer. He was taller than Tully, every bit as brash, and from something he'd said earlier, Noah already knew he was Irish. "A free meal every time we show up, ya say? And a coat to boot?"

"That's right."

The boy eyed Noah as if he were an object less than worthy of consideration. Even though his height was in his favor, bulk was not. He was as scrawny as a scarecrow.

"I'll be there."

To Noah's vague surprise, four of the nine boys told him they would be at the first rehearsal the night after next. But not Tully.

Now all he had to do was share the news with the

pastor—and hope he'd meant it when he'd said he wanted to show the love of God to those outside the church.

Noah figured he couldn't get much further outside the church than the boys he was about to bring in.

Chapter 6

"I don't see why we can't just ask fully grown men from our church to fill the roles in the pageant." Was Sophie the only one wondering such a thing? It appeared so, since even Alice, next to her, looked at her with some surprise.

"The point is to invite others in," Noah said, "so you can get to know some of your new neighbors."

His gaze was settled firmly on Sophie's, once again with a light in his eyes. The man was actually proud of himself! But why wouldn't he be, if he was intent on bringing in boys just like the one he'd been himself—a rascal and a scamp?

Sophie could hardly believe both of her parents were so agreeable to a plan Noah had obviously concocted all on his own. Even though the pastor had presented the idea of a choir and pageant to the church on Sunday, he'd just now given the credit to Noah for the promise of a successful pageant. If she'd known it was Noah's idea, she wouldn't have come to this first planning meeting at all.

"The boys will always be supervised," Pastor Goodwin reminded everyone. "Noah has agreed to direct, so he'll be here for every rehearsal. My wife will conduct the music, and Mr. Stewart will take care of the nativity scenery while his good wife will see to the costumes and our new choir robes."

"And the coats and promised meals?" Sophie asked. "Where will the provisions come from?"

"I'm sure every family will be happy to donate an item or two," Pastor Goodwin said, adding with a grin, "I've been told you make the best beef stew this side of the Mississippi, Sophie."

"That's true," chimed her mother.

Alice, next to Sophie, leaned close and whispered in Sophie's ear. "Aren't you tired of playing the grumbler every time Noah has anything to do with something? Go ahead and agree!"

Sophie knew she couldn't very well refuse, not unless she wanted it to be assumed her faith in mankind was so lacking she didn't want to help feed a few hungry boys. She *must* agree, even if it was for a bunch of rapscallions led by the Pied Piper of brutes himself.

"Actually, I was hoping for more help from Sophie—Miss Stewart." Noah corrected himself the way he used to when in the presence of polite company. For heaven's sake, he'd been calling her Sophie ever since she could remember! "I was hoping she might help with rehearsals. If she's up to the challenge, of course."

All eyes, not just Noah's, now rested on her. She was to be dared in public to participate in something that might very well be an impossible task, at Noah Jackson's side? Working with scoundrels who were likely every bit as much trouble as Noah had once been?

"I think that's a wonderful idea, dear," her mother announced. "After all, Gordy will be involved, and you've always gotten on so well with him and boys his age."

Who didn't get along with good boys? But this was altogether different. She'd already opened her mouth to agree to cook a meal or two, and somewhere along the way she'd clamped it shut. It wasn't until Alice nudged her that she realized she must open her mouth again, no matter what kind of alarm clanged inside her head.

"Yes, of course I want our church program to be wonderful. I'll help." Then she eyed Alice, who was smiling so smugly that Sophie added, "And I'm sure Alice will be happy to assist, too."

Alice's brows rose in surprise, but she smiled and

agreed when Arthur took her hand from her other side. "We'll both help," he said, holding up the hand he clasped.

That was some comfort. At least she wouldn't have to spend the evenings ahead as the only nonrascal in the room.

❦

Midway through the first rehearsal, Noah was beginning to wonder if his plan would succeed. It had started so promisingly, despite only one boy beside Gordy coming from the church. All four of the street boys showed up.

That was when Sophie's face became more guarded than ever. How was he to convince her that even rascals could change?

Not helping matters was his greatest challenge so far—not from the street boys, but from Sally Hobson.

"But I only came to help with the dinner because Alice told me to come," Sally said.

"Don't you want to be part of the pageant, Sally?"

And then, to his surprise, Sophie came to his aid. "Especially in such an important role? Other than the baby Jesus, who is more important than Mary?"

The girl wrung her hands. "Well. . .I never thought I could get up in front of others and. . .act."

"Oh for heaven's sake, Sally," said Alice, who evidently found it unnecessary to exhibit much patience with her little sister, "you're the right age and size. And besides, we have no one else. You'll have to do it."

Sophie reached out to caution her friend's tone, but it was Noah who lightened the mood with a laugh.

"How can anyone resist such a persuasive request?" Then he looked at Sally. "You might want to consider that at present our only alternative is to dress up one of the boys as Mary—"

"Hey!" cried Louie, one of the boys from the street. "We ain't none of us gonna put on a dress. Them shepherd robes is close 'nough."

To Noah's relief, he saw the hint of a smile hover at the corners of Sally's lips.

"Half the boys here are starting to sprout whiskers." Noah added a grin to his coaxing. "I don't think Mary would like to be portrayed by any of them. What do you think, Sally?"

The smile broke free at last, and she nodded.

"Thank you, Sally. Or should I call you Mary?"

∞

Was Sophie the only one immune to Noah Jackson's charm? He was like a chameleon she'd read of, a little creature able to change its colors whenever necessary.

Eyeing the boys who had come to participate, she couldn't help but remember the compassion she'd felt watching them eat, as if none of them had tasted such a meal in their lives. Although they expressed no gratitude other than finishing every last bit of the stew she'd provided, and every one of them used his shirtsleeves to wipe off his hands and mouth, she had to admit they were less threatening than she expected. None of them seemed to be carrying a slingshot, or worse.

Her greatest surprise of the evening came with how the boys treated Gordy—as if they'd known each other forever. Her mother had certainly been right to be concerned. Only when they teased him about playing the angel did she find herself less worried; at least they thought only Gordy could fit such a role.

After Noah described how the nativity play would unfold, other roles were offered and decided. Most of the boys were to be shepherds, while Gordy would, at least for now, double as both the angel and one of the three kings. The other two kings would be played by one of the street boys and by Arthur, whose height—or lack of it—allowed him to pass as one of the boys.

"The shepherds are frightened at first," Noah explained. "After all, wouldn't you be if you saw someone coming down from the skies and talking to you?"

Louie laughed and jabbed the boy next to him. "Not if Lorcan swiped his daddy's whiskey jug again. We'd see all kinds of things and wouldn't be afraid neither."

Noah laughed right along with the boys, but Sophie frowned. Didn't his laugh encourage such harmful behavior?

"But they're also curious," Noah went on. "These brave shepherds. Instead of cowering or running home to hide from something they'd never seen before, they follow the angel's instructions. They go to Bethlehem, where they find the proof of what the angel told them. That's where they adore the Savior of the world." He looked around at the boys then added softly, "Our Savior, too. Mine and yours.

"So we'll begin with a narrator," he went on. "That's Pastor Goodwin. He'll speak from behind a curtain, so everyone will hear him but not see him. He'll start by telling everyone about Herod and the wise men and the reason Joseph must take Mary to Bethlehem to be counted in the census. . . ."

He continued to explain the roles, even citing their lines, having them repeat them, and asking them to remember what to say for the coming rehearsals. It would have been far easier had he distributed a script of some kind, and Sophie was determined to ask him about it just as soon as the rehearsal ended. Surely Alice would help Sophie copy such a thing.

"And when the host of angels join our angel—Gordy—we'll have the choir lead everyone in the song 'Hark! The Herald Angels Sing.' That way the audience can be part of the pageant. Afterward, with the shepherds looking on, the three wise men appear with their gifts, and they, too, worship the baby Jesus. Then the angel returns, telling the wise men to go home by a different route and not tell Herod about Jesus. He also tells Joseph to take Mary and the baby out of Bethlehem, to safety, and that ends the pageant: with Mary looking back on the scene while the choir sings 'Christians Awake! On This Happy Morn.' "

"Are we gonna have to sing, too?" asked Flynn, the boy standing next to Gordy. Earlier he'd seemed happy to be a shepherd, but he didn't look particularly interested in singing.

"We'll all sing," said Mrs. Goodwin. "We might even have a piano by then! The church's first Christmas present, from a wonderful benefactor named Ezra Pooley."

The familiar name made Sophie's gaze dart from the pastor's wife to Noah, who wasn't even looking her way, for once. Instead, he put a hand on the concerned boy's shoulder. "We'll have plenty of time to learn our lines and the songs, too. We'll start tonight with the songs. Okay, Flynn?"

"Don't worry about your voice, Flynn," added Arthur. "I only sing loud enough for God to hear. I figure He gave me a voice that can't hold a tune, so He must somehow like it. But I'm not sure anybody else wants to hear it." He looked Alice's way, who beamed so fondly no one could have doubted she'd welcome his voice, no matter how off-key.

Sophie wondered what it must be like to have someone so blind to one's faults.

Sometime later, after the boys had departed, Noah asked Sophie if he could escort her home.

"No, it's not necessary," she said. "Arthur is coming along because Alice lives so close."

Noah nodded without trying to change her mind, and turned away. So much for being a persistent suitor! She called him back.

"If you have a script," she said, "I can copy it for the boys if you like."

"No scripts. No sheet music. Nothing that requires reading."

She tilted her head. "Why ever not? It would be much easier—"

"Because half the boys who came tonight can't read. I'm hoping they are, even now, boasting about full bellies, how warm the church is, and how easy the practice was. We need another wise man and more angels. A whole host of them. We're not going to bring any more boys in if we don't spare their pride."

He crossed the three steps separating them, stopping only when his face was closer to hers than necessary. "Because most of life's problems can be traced to pride, in one form or another."

Pride? Was he accusing her of being prideful? Or confessing his own?

"And you think the rest of the angels will come from the streets?" Somehow, the question wasn't issued with the same disdainful disbelief she might have used before tonight's rehearsal.

"That's right."

His confidence made her wonder if he might just be right, after all.

Chapter 7

"I don't see why you won't let Noah take you to see Mr. Pooley, that's all."

Arthur walked beside Sophie, setting a brisk pace toward Mr. Pooley's home that he'd said was on Lake Street. For a hopefully leisurely visit with his older friend, Arthur didn't look at all relaxed.

"And while we're on the subject of Noah—"

So that was the reason for his scowl. Noah again. "That's your subject, Arthur. Not mine."

"That's just it. I guess I understood back in Toledo why you might have run the other way when you caught sight of him, but he was a kid then, and so were you. Can't you see he's changed?"

"How do you restore something that's rotten inside? He may have learned how to polish the outside, but who can say he's any different on the inside?"

"I can! You don't share the same roof with somebody for five years and not know him. Sure, he used to play pranks. But once he got a job—a real job that paid, not the kind his parents made him do without so much as a thank-you—he turned his energy to good, hard work."

Sophie harrumphed and kept walking. "Just look at the kids he's brought to the nativity. They're all exactly like him—how he used to be. Every one of those boys reminds me of who Noah is on the inside."

"Those boys have changed in just three weeks. They laugh *with* each other now instead of *at* each other. They encourage one another." He grinned. "I even saw one of them use a napkin instead of his shirtsleeve."

"You can't make a silk purse out of a sow's ear, Arthur."

Arthur stopped and grabbed her shoulders. "You're proof that someone can change, Sophie. You used to be sweet. But now your heart is hard." His fingers squeezed her shoulders, as if in frustration. Then he let her go. "I've changed my mind about today's visit. If you want to see Mr. Pooley's copy of that bird book, you're going to have to ask Noah for the introduction."

Then he turned and walked in the opposite direction.

"Arthur!"

But her brother ignored her call.

Sophie had no choice but to make her way back home. As much as she wanted to see—to study, admire, even emulate—the drawings of such an eminent artist as Mr. Wilson, she would not suffer Noah Jackson's company to do so.

❧

Noah eyed Tully. He'd been right about him from the first, that he was a leader, if not the top of the bunch. Several other new boys had come tonight, too, but Noah hadn't expected Tully.

"We could use another shepherd," Noah said slowly.

"Shepherd!" echoed Gordy. "He can have my spot as the third wise man, since I'm already the angel."

Noah hesitated as everyone looked at him expectantly, including Tully. Clearly they all recognized the boy's dominance and were ready to give him a prized role. Noah couldn't say exactly what he didn't trust about this boy, but a definite alarm bell sounded in his soul.

His alarm might be similar to the one ringing in Sophie's soul about him—an alarm that was groundless, based on feeling, not fact. If he believed people could change, he'd have to believe Tully could, too. So Noah patted the boy's shoulder.

"Good to have you join us, Tully. A wise man it is then."

Eying Sophie, he couldn't help but see the disapproval on her face. Tully was just one more boy to her, one more to add to the list of delinquents working on this pageant.

He looked again at Tully, who playfully punched Gordy on the arm—a little too hard, perhaps, but in their language, a sign of gratitude for a preferred role. The rest of the boys were coming around, he was sure of it. By Christmas Eve when they presented the nativity pageant, even Sophie would have to admit the boys showed promise—particularly if the apprenticeships and jobs Noah was working to secure came through.

But Tully? If Noah had to guess, this latecomer would need the most amount of change to reform, and Noah feared it might already be too late for time to be on his side with this one. At least to convince Sophie that all boys deserved a second chance.

By the middle of the evening, Noah was more worried than ever. In a single night, Tully managed to reignite all of the disruptive behavior Noah had successfully curbed in the past weeks. Like the leader he was, Tully's example of amusing ridicule spurred the others into matching tones—all in the name of fun.

He put an end to it when Tully teased Sally. Noah didn't hear the exact words, but given the crimson in Sally's cheeks and the horror on Gordy's face, it evidently had something to do with wanting to take the

Holy Spirit's place the next time "Mary" was with child.

"That's enough, Tully," Noah said. "You haven't had the advantage the other boys have had, working together these last few weeks. We've made it clear this isn't just a performance for the church. It's portraying a holy memory. If you have no desire to act with respect for what we're doing, then I'll ask you to leave. Understood?"

The apology on Tully's face looked so sincere Noah wished he could believe him. But the boy's behavior had reminded him all too clearly of why Sophie remained wary of him, even after all these years. He'd given a few apologies like this himself back in his youth. All show and no truth.

Noah was exhausted. Working with the railroad commission all day and coming to the rehearsals in the evenings had been exhilarating until tonight. Back at his lodgings with Arthur, his feet dragged all the way up the stairs and to his cot.

In spite of that—or maybe because he knew it offered comfort—he pulled out the leatherwork tools he'd borrowed from Ezra then turned up the oil lamp beside his cot.

"Why are you doing all this anyway?" Arthur asked, watching him work.

"What do you mean?"

"I know you started out wanting to win over Sophie, but is it worth it? All she does is turn up her nose at you. She's my sister, and I know she can be good-natured, and I'll take your word that she's pretty enough, but is she worth all this trouble? Maybe she's not meant to get married, or maybe she's meant to marry somebody else."

"You might be right, Artie," Noah said, without pause in his work. "Except the truth is, I started falling in love with her as far back as reading some of those letters she wrote to you. So it's your fault. You shouldn't have shared them with me."

Arthur lay back on his cot. "All right then. Love's a whole different story. I just hope you can bring back the sweet sister she was in those letters."

Chapter 8

Sophie arrived early at church on Christmas Eve, hearing the excited voices of the boys who would perform tonight. Eager to join them, she stopped briefly in the coatroom to hang her coat—only to see a note tacked beneath the peg she always used.

Curious, she unfolded what looked like official stationary. Scrawled across the top, just below the address labeling it from a local newspaper, were written the bold words: *Merry Christmas, Sophie, but this isn't really a gift since your talent earned the chance.*

Breath quickened, Sophie read the body of the letter. It was an invitation to submit her wildlife drawings to the editor at Chicago's *Prairie Farmer*.

Amazed, she looked around, wondering where the note had come from. Arthur, who was just hanging his own coat, was the only one nearby.

"Look at this!"

He took the page from her, scanning it briefly as a smile grew on his face. "That's Noah's writing at the top."

She gasped. "Do. . . Do you think this is a prank?"

Her brother moaned and scrubbed his face from hair to chin. "It'd serve you right to pass up the opportunity you want most in the world because you can't believe Noah has changed."

Then he waved a hand of disgust at her and went off in search of Alice.

∾

"Fear not! For behold, I bring you good tidings of great joy, which shall be to all people. . . ."

Sophie watched Gordy from the audience, stealing a glance from him to their parents and seeing every bit as much pride on their faces as she felt in her heart. Although the pageant had just begun, it was already a success. The entire cast had shown up, even that rascal Tully, and she felt confident Gordy wasn't the only one who knew his lines.

And the church was filled! There might be more taverns, brothels, and gambling dens in Chicago than there were churches, but on Christmas Eve it appeared even the hardest of hearts turned a little soft when it came to remembering the Christ child.

Although Sophie couldn't see Noah, she easily imagined him behind the makeshift curtains, ensuring everyone went on and off the improvised stage at the appropriate time. If her heart had swelled upon hearing her brother's sweet recitation of an angel's invitation to the shepherds, that same heart pounded anew over how hard Noah had worked on this evening's performance. All of it had been his vision, right down to the players involved.

She'd doubted him, she couldn't deny it. But every one of the boys she'd so easily mistrusted had turned out to be similar to Gordy—eager to be accepted, ready to learn his part and to help someone else when necessary. She'd seen them filled with energy and brimming with laughter—in fact, looking for something to laugh about. How could that not be contagious?

Most surprising was Tully, the latecomer she was sure would put a damper on everything. But there he was, the third wise man, offering myrrh and worshipping Mary's babe. Noah may not have accomplished such a miracle, but certainly God couldn't have done it without his cooperation. And that was a miracle, too. The heart she believed so dark inside of Noah had been washed clean. Who was she to have doubted God could do such a thing for him?

All that was left now was regret that she'd clung so long to her mistrust of him. How could she not have seen that he believed in her drawings enough to arrange for the opportunity to be published in a real city newspaper?

O come, all ye faithful
Joyful and triumphant,
O come ye, O come ye, to Bethlehem.

Sophie joined the singing with adoration, knowing that God had reminded her not only of His love, but also to trust another's love—one she'd been fighting too long.

Noah's heart hadn't been the only one in need of a washing. Her own had been too suspicious, too judgmental, too timid to realize that if she only trusted God's work in Noah, she would have admitted weeks ago she was falling in love with him.

As the pageant came to a close, applause echoed from the rafters. No one clapped louder than Sophie as she searched the edges of the stage for a glimpse of the man who had inspired the entire evening.

∽

Noah hadn't realized the extent of his own fidgetiness until the audience burst into cheers at the end of the performance. He breathed freely for the first time that evening. There hadn't been a single blunder, if he didn't count Louie dropping the gold-painted stones at the foot of the crèche. Even Mrs. Gutierrez's baby, just five weeks old, had been quiet through the entire performance as if in reverence to his part as the baby Jesus.

As the cast returned behind the scenes, he congratulated each of them while the crowd filed out. With some disappointment, he noticed Sophie talking with her parents as they approached the door at the other end of the sanctuary. Knowing they were leaving dashed his hopes that she might have stayed, but he comforted himself, knowing he would see her tomorrow.

Some of the cast had agreed to stay late to clean up so the church would be ready for Christmas morning service. As he folded costumes, he realized Gordy was among those who had stayed, and his pulse leaped with the thought of seeing Sophie again if he took the boy safely home.

"It turned out beautifully, Noah."

The quiet, familiar voice from the dimmed sanctuary nearly made him drop the shepherd's robe.

Sophie.

Had her voice sounded nearly breathless? He took a careful step closer to her, knowing he was too eager to hope he was responsible for taking her breath away. But the way she looked at him doubled his pulse.

"It turned out well, didn't it?"

"It's a memory that will live in the heart of everyone who was here tonight." She spoke with a shyness he hadn't seen in her since they were children. "At least I know it will always be in my heart."

Her smile went so clearly beyond her lips that he nearly approached her for a kiss. But he was too stunned to even try.

"Will it?" he asked instead, knowing he was apt to believe what he wanted with the slightest hint of hope. She was the last person he wanted to frighten away.

"Noah." Was he fooling himself to hear something new in her voice? Surely she'd never called him by name so invitingly. "You arranged for me to submit my drawings to the *Prairie Farmer*, didn't you?"

"I told you they're good. They thought so, too, when I showed them the ones you sent to Artie."

"Oh Noah. . .I don't know how to thank you."

"You're welcome, but all I did was present the pictures. Your work did the rest."

The look in her eye multiplied the hope in his heart, and he dared another step closer, setting the robe on a nearby bench.

"I'm sorry I've been so foolish." She, too, stepped nearer, whispering the words as if they were alone, even though a few others still lingered. "About everything. Those boys were remarkable tonight. I was so wrong to think they couldn't be touched by God's love—and the love you showed them."

"Don't think too highly of me," he said. "I tried convincing myself I did it for Gordy, because I knew he was hanging around some of these boys. I know God loves them all and they needed to be shown that. But the truth is, I was trying to impress you with how much I've changed."

To his relief, his confessions didn't erase her smile. "I think God used you in spite of me. And you let Him. I was an idiot not to see that."

Noah could no longer keep himself in check. Who would be shocked if he kissed her right here, right now? The boys would likely cheer him on. And Pastor Goodwin had surely seen the way he'd been looking at her from the moment she arrived in town.

But no sooner had his lips brushed hers than he heard the door burst open and a scuffle at the threshold.

Chapter 9

Awash with confusion, Sophie had been about to pull Noah closer when he shot away, running toward a noise at the back of the small church sanctuary. Just beyond the last pew she saw three boys tussling—Louie and Lorcan appeared to be dragging a struggling Tully back inside the church. Then Lorcan ripped open Tully's brand-new coat. Buttons tapped on the floor—along with a thud and jingle from a box landing a few feet away.

The boys behind her all raised their voices at once, whether in support of the fight or against it, she couldn't tell. Lorcan still had a grip on Tully's coat while Louie ducked clear of Tully's fist. The boy freed himself just as Noah came up from behind, grabbing Tully's arms in a stronghold. When Lorcan looked as if he might take another swing at the hog-tied enemy, Sophie cried out as Noah pulled Tully safely beyond the reach of Lorcan's punching arm.

"That's enough!" Noah shouted, Tully still imprisoned. "What's this about?"

Gordy picked up the box that had fallen during the fight. "This is the collection box!"

Pastor Goodwin stepped forward, reaching for the box. "It certainly is. I'd put it under my coat while I was helping with the cleanup."

"Here's the rat that took it!" Lorcan yelled at Tully. "I told you we weren't going in on that scheme—"

Sophie came up beside Gordy. "Scheme? Did you know about a scheme, Gordy?"

He shook his head.

"Well, I did," said Louie. "So did half the other fellas. Only we all tol' him we wasn't gonna do it— distract ever'body so he could get away with it."

"I didn't see him take it, but I guess he gone and done it anyway," Lorcan added.

Tully had the good sense to hang his head, because not one of his fellow street boys looked as if they'd offer him a smidgeon of compassion.

<hr>

Noah could have moaned aloud. So much for redemption. He couldn't help but wonder if Sophie believed a bully's heart was destined to remain one, just as, it seemed, was Tully's.

He'd been so close to winning her this evening. He'd seen it in her face. He nearly didn't want to see her now, for fear her light of faith had been stamped out.

So he looked at the pastor instead. "Do you want me to turn the boy over to the constable?"

Pastor Goodwin approached Tully. "We all must take responsibility for our actions, son. Do you know that what you did was wrong?"

Tully nodded, still looking at the floor.

"Look up, son. Look at the faces of the boys who used to respect you."

The guilty boy didn't look up, and Noah adjusted his grip with a shake. "Go on."

Tully raised his head and looked at the pastor. "They're all a bunch o' mice, and I don't care what they think o' me. What's gonna happen now this is over? We all go back to empty bellies, that's what. I only took what we needed. New coats ain't gonna feed us."

"What about the jobs I'm working on for some of you?" Noah asked.

"Some of us! Not for me!"

"We weren't going to abandon you now that the nativity is over," Pastor Goodwin said. "We want all of you to keep coming to church."

Noah increased his grip. "Didn't it occur to you that stealing isn't exactly the best way to get a good recommendation for a job?"

Tully only shrugged.

Noah exchanged a look with the pastor, and he could see the man was already willing to offer grace. But Noah wasn't eager to do so—either to prove to Sophie he saw her point about bullies or because the boy might have spoiled his own chances with her. He was still afraid to look at her for fear of seeing ready condemnation, but she stepped into his line of vision.

She eyed the boy still imprisoned by Noah's grip, staring at him until he met her gaze. At first she frowned, just the way Noah would have expected. Then, to his fascination, her frown softened into a look of pure concern.

"Is it true you took the money to help feed the others? Or did you take it for yourself?"

"Whatever I say you won't believe anyway."

"That's probably true. Which is why you'll need time to prove yourself." She looked at Noah now. "But I'm not sure the stockade is the place to do that."

"You can have a job here at the church," Pastor Goodwin said. "Sweeping the floors, dusting the benches. Cleaning up inside and out. It won't pay much, but you could sleep in the coatroom and have dinners with Mrs. Goodwin and me. But"—he looked at the rest of the boys—"I'll need help from each of you. If there is a next time, I'll want to know in advance if young Mr. Tully has any trouble up his sleeve. It's not tattling if you have his best interest in mind."

Noah couldn't tear his gaze from Sophie even to look at Tully, whom he was sure was relieved over the pastor's verdict. Instead, Noah marveled at the compassion in Sophie's eyes—confirming she believed in second chances.

⁓∞⁓

"But I didn't get you anything!"

Sophie stood in front of Noah, who had just arrived at her parents' house this early Christmas morning. Her mother was in the kitchen, where Sophie should be helping. But when Noah had arrived—without Arthur, who had told them he would go to Alice's for Christmas morning—Sophie's father had called her out of the kitchen so soon after the knock, she was sure Noah hadn't even announced who he'd come to see.

Abandoned by both Gordy and her father, who had left them for the kitchen, Noah stood before her with a flat box, complete with a silk ribbon tying it closed.

"You already gave me exactly what I wanted this Christmas," Noah told her. "Hope. That's hard to wrap, but just as real as what I have for you. Now open it."

They sat near the small Christmas tree that she and Gordy had decorated with popcorn and cranberries, its trunk skirted by a circle of linen she had embroidered with a nativity scene last year. Little had she known it was bound to remind her of Noah!

She had to steady her hands to untie the ribbon before opening the box. He'd taken special care to wrap the present inside with a layer of cloth. The scent of leather greeted her immediately, and she shot him a smile.

"Did you make this?"

He nodded.

Uncovering the gift, she saw it was a book bound at the side with another ribbon. The cover made her gasp. It was intricately tooled with the images of birds. Carefully, she opened to the few pages within, surprised to find her own drawings.

"Oh Noah," she whispered. "It's for my drawings, isn't it?"

"They're the ones you sent to Artie, the ones I showed to the *Prairie Farmer* editor. You can add new ones as you create them. See?" He pulled the ribbon. "It comes apart. When you're finished, I can have it bound, just like a real book."

"Oh Noah." She knew she'd repeated herself but

was nearly overcome with happiness. "It's so beautiful."

Then she looked at the cover again. "These birds. . . My goodness, Noah. They're so well done."

"I can't take credit for the artwork. I'm not an artist like you are. Mr. Pooley gave me a few tissue paper leaflets from one of his bird books, and I traced the smallest pictures and placed it on top of my leather. Then I pressed my pencil into it so I could follow the image with my etching tool. See?" He pointed to each bird as he spoke. "That's a partridge, and a turtledove next to it. And the hen is French, of course." He laughed. "And that other one is a calling bird, but you have to use your imagination."

"Oh Noah, it's the perfect Christmas present."

"That's the best carol for you, Sophie. 'The Twelve Days of Christmas.' What other carol has so many birds in it? The other verses are on the back, the ones without birds. I traced most of those images from children's books at the library. I went almost every day, hoping to see you there."

She turned the book over, seeing images of the remaining verses, each meticulously if roughly etched in the smooth, stained leather.

All verses but one.

"And where are the five golden rings?" she asked.

"Look inside the back cover. That was the easiest for me to etch."

She opened the book reverently, because her drawings were housed with such obvious love. A flap at the back would easily hold pencils and a knife for sharpening, but it bulged too slightly now for that. The folded top was decorated in the image of five rings.

"Open it."

Exploring inside, she caught her breath before gently pulling out a ring.

"I'll put it on your finger just as soon as you let Pastor Goodwin marry us. See? It's five strands of gold—five golden rings—all entwined together. For your wedding ring."

Noah put his hands over hers. "Will you marry me, Sophie?"

She laughed, throwing her arms around his neck. "Yes, Noah! I'm to be a bride, after all—yours!"

Stew and Dumplings

1 pound chuck, tip, or round steak cut into 1 inch cubes

1 tablespoon butter

3 cups chicken or beef stock

½ teaspoon salt

⅛ teaspoon pepper

2 medium carrots, cut into 1 inch pieces

2 large potatoes (approximately 2 cups), cut into 1 inch pieces

1 small onion, chopped

Melt butter in large saucepan or Dutch oven. Add beef and cook until browned, approximately 15 minutes. Add stock and salt and pepper. Heat to a boil, then reduce heat and simmer for 2 hours. Stir in cut carrots, potatoes, and onion. Add ½ cup cold water and 2 tablespoons flour. Stir to blend. Heat to a boil again, approximately 1 minute. Reduce heat and simmer 30 minutes to allow vegetables to cook.

Dumplings:

1½ cups flour

2 teaspoons baking powder

¾ teaspoon salt

3 tablespoons shortening

½ cup milk

Cut shortening into flour as you would for a pie crust. Add baking powder and salt, stir, then add milk. Dough will be wet. Drop dumplings by spoonfuls on top of stew. Cook uncovered for 10 minutes, then cover and cook for 10 minutes more. Uncover and serve.

Recipe compliments of Lora Haapapuro.

About the Author

Maureen Lang writes stories inspired by a love of history and romance. An avid reader herself, she's figured out a way to write the stories she feels like reading. Maureen's Inspirationals have earned various writing distinctions including the Inspirational Readers Choice Contenst, a Holt Medallion, and the Selah Award, as well as being a finalist for the Rita, Christy, and Carol Awards. In addition to investigating various eras in history (such as Victorian England, First World War, and America's Gilded Age), Maureen loves taking research trips to get a feel for the settings of her novels. She lives in the Chicago area with her family and has been blessed to be the primary caregiver to her adult disabled son.

The Gingerbread Bride

by Amy Lillard

Chapter 1

Ozark Mountains, Arkansas, 1870

"Madeline!"

Maddie Sinclair winced at the sharpness in her sister's tone. Grace slammed through the house they shared with their father and burst into the kitchen before Maddie could do so much as hike her skirt and run for the stairs. At least she managed to pull off her soiled apron and toss it into the sink.

"There you are." Grace's cheeks were stained pink from the Christmas Eve cold and what Maddie could only assume was the excursion of running her down in the kitchen.

"Of course this is where I am." Maddie smoothed the front of her day dress, dismayed at the smear of flour on the bodice. And was that one across her nose? She crossed her eyes to check and swiped at it just to be certain.

"You did it, didn't you?"

"Did what?" She could never keep Grace from finding out the truth. It had been that way since they were children. Her imitation innocence would only take her so far this time.

Her sister propped her hands on her hips and narrowed her gaze. "Annie Johnson at the general store said she saw you headed out toward Old Lady Farley's place yesterday."

Maddie sniffed. "I don't see how that's a problem."

"It became a problem when Pa told me that Harlan Calhoun was coming to dinner tonight."

At the mention of Harlan's name, Maddie couldn't stop the smile that spread across her face. "Of course Harlan is coming to dinner tonight. It is Christmas Eve, after all. And he doesn't have any kin near. It's only the Christian thing to do, invite him to supper."

"You're stalling," Gracie said. "A sure sign that you're up to something. Now, what about Old Lady Farley?"

Maddie took a steadying breath. She could do this. "I don't know what you're talking about, sister."

"So you're telling me that you didn't go see Old Lady Farley to get something to make Harlan Calhoun fall in love with you?"

Maddie scoffed, sort of choked, but managed to recover. She never should have mentioned her thoughts aloud. Especially not to her practical and perfect sibling. "Why, that's ridiculous."

Some of the starch melted out of Gracie's spine. She smiled. "That's what I was hoping you would say." She inhaled deeply. "What's that I smell?"

Maddie gestured toward two plates of freshly baked gingerbread cookies.

"You made cookies?"

"A special treat for a special day." She pushed the larger plate toward Gracie. "These are for the family." She lifted the smaller plate. "And these here are for Harlan."

"Maddie." There was that warning note back in her sister's tone.

Maddie shrugged as a knock sounded on the door. "I want him to feel special."

"Maddie."

Maddie patted down her hair and pinched a bit of color into her cheeks. Then before her sister could make a move, she swept toward the parlor, a plate of cookies in her hands.

Harlan Calhoun was twirling his hat in his hands as he was prone to do. He always seemed a bit nervous when he came by their house, but Maddie didn't know why. He walked with confidence every time she saw him in their tiny town of Calico Falls in the foothills of the Ozark Mountains. Harlan had moved to their town in the spring, and Maddie had fallen immediately in love. He was tall and handsome, gentlemanly, and had a city air about him that her Arkansas suitors could never achieve. But it was more than that. He was God fearing and Lord loving, and she so desperately wanted to marry him.

She smiled as she cleared her throat, alerting him to her presence. "Merry Christmas, Harlan." Her cheeks grew hot with the use of his Christian name. He had told her a few weeks ago that she should call him Harlan, but this was the first time she had managed to squeeze the word through her lips when addressing him.

"And a merry Christmas Eve to you as well, Miss Maddie." He swept into a deep bow.

"I made you some gingerbread cookies to enjoy before supper." Her voice trembled as she said the words. Had he noticed? "Why don't you sit down, and I'll get you a glass of milk. Unless you'd rather have coffee."

He smiled, the action lighting the entire room. "Milk would be fine indeed." He folded his tall frame into the parlor chair. He looked ridiculously handsome in the tiny seat. Big and capable and handsome. So handsome.

Maddie set the cookies on the table next to him and sucked in a quick breath. "I'll just go. . .get the milk." She backed out of the room, never taking her eyes from Harlan as she pushed through the swinging door that led into the kitchen.

"Maddie!" her sister whispered, urgency tainting her words. "What is this?" She held up the tiny linen sack Maddie had thought she'd hidden where no one would find it.

Maddie snatched it away from Grace and tucked it behind her. "Nothing."

"You did something to those cookies. Don't even bother lying about it."

Maddie sighed, her resolve slipping. It was wrong to lie. Just as she knew that what she'd planned for Harlan wasn't the most. . .conventional method of finding a husband. "I had to, Gracie. How else am I supposed to make him fall in love with me?" The words rang between them with a hollow sound. What had she done?

"Maddie." Gracie shook her head.

"I'm not like you," Maddie said, hating the envious edge in her voice. Her sister was poised and polished, as beautiful as their dearly departed mother and twice as sweet. Maddie could never win when compared with her only sibling. Once, just once, she wanted something special of her own.

Harlan Calhoun.

"You can't do that to the poor man," her sister gently said.

"But I love him."

"So it's okay to poison him so he'll propose to you?"

Maddie sniffed. "I think he likes me well enough."

Grace shook her head. "You have to get out there and get those cookies."

Maddie knew it to be true before her sister uttered the first syllable. As much as she hated to, as much as she desperately wanted Harlan's love, it wasn't right. Not like this. She nodded.

Grace nudged her toward the door. "Now, before he eats them."

Spurred into action, Maddie hustled through the door and back into the parlor.

Harlan stood as she entered, brushing the crumbs from his mouth. He swallowed hard, his lips twitching into a small smile. "I thought you were bringing milk."

"I, uh, was," she hedged, her gaze darting to the plate. Empty! "Did you, uh, eat the cookies?" She knew the answer but had to ask.

"I skipped lunch and then. . ." He gave her a sheepish smile. "Well, they were delicious."

Her heart sank in her chest, but she forced a smile. "I'm glad you enjoyed them."

"I did. Very much so." His deep blue eyes turned suddenly serious. "Listen, Maddie. I came here tonight for a very important reason."

She licked her lips, her throat suddenly dry. "You did?" she whispered.

He grabbed her hands and dropped to one knee.

Oh goodness! She hadn't expected it to work this fast.

"Harlan," she exclaimed before he could utter the one question she wanted to hear above all else. "Stand up. What's wrong with you?" Like she didn't know.

"I love you, Maddie."

She had been waiting to hear those words from him ever since he arrived in Calico Falls, and now it was nothing more than a lie. The biggest part of her heart wanted to ignore the voice of her conscience, the one that told her this was all wrong, and drop to her knees beside him.

Instead, she tugged him to his feet. "Now, Harlan, is that any way to treat your fine suit?" She resisted the urge to brush her hands across his lapels. That would be too forward. As much as her fingers itched to dance over his broad chest, it would be best to ignore that impulse until he was back to himself. Or not give in to it at all.

"Maddie, it's just that I want to—"

She shook her head. "Give me one moment. I need to get you that milk." It was the worst excuse, but the only one she could think of.

"I wouldn't mind another cookie or two." He grinned at her.

"Oh, I think you've had quite enough cookies." She scooped up the empty plate and hustled from the room.

Grace was waiting on the other side of the kitchen door. "Well?"

Maddie held out the cookie plate.

"He ate all of them?"

She nodded.

"*All* of them?"

"Do you see any left?"

"Madeline Joy, don't you get all snippy with me. This wasn't my harebrained idea."

Maddie's irritation wilted. "I'm sorry, Grace. Forgive me. It's just that—"

"What?" her sister asked.

"I've waited for this for so long, and now I've gone and ruined it." Tears rose to her eyes. "What am I supposed to do?"

Grace pulled her close. "Shh. . .don't cry. We'll think of something." Grace gave her one more squeeze and let her go. "Now, how long did Old Lady Farley say this would last?"

"She didn't say." Maddie sniffed.

"So you did drug the cookies."

Maddie nodded. "It's just some harmless herbs and spices. I would never hurt him."

"Only make him fall in love with you against his will."

"Oh Grace," she cried. "What am I going to do?"

Her sister gently pushed the door open to peek into the parlor. "You're going to go out there and keep him occupied so he can't ask Pa for your hand in marriage."

Maddie swallowed hard but nodded. Then she smoothed down her dress and pushed the escaped strands of her hair back into place.

"Here." Grace thrust a cool glass of milk into her hands. "Now go out there and keep him busy."

❧

Harlan Jay Calhoun watched the door that Maddie disappeared behind and waited for her return. He hadn't meant to scare her, but he had been holding in his feelings for so very long. She looked particularly beautiful today. He should be used to that by now. Every time he saw her she seemed even lovelier than she had the time before. But here, today, on Christmas Eve, she nearly took his breath away.

And how had he repaid her? He'd stuffed down her cookies like they were nothing. But they were just so good. And he was hungry and nervous.

He touched the box tucked safely in the inside pocket of his jacket. He had waited two months for the treasured cameo to arrive from his parents' house in the East. How else was he supposed to ask Maddie to be his wife? He had to give her something special. Yet he had been so nervous since he'd picked it up from the post office two days ago. It had taken that long to gather up courage enough to come over here and ask for her hand.

Now all he had to do was wait for her to come out of the kitchen.

He breathed a sigh of relief when she swung into the room a few moments later. What had he expected her to do? Not come back at all?

"There you are," he said. He rushed toward her, unable to stop his feet from carrying him directly to her side. He had been denying his feelings for so long, waiting until the right time to tell her that he loved her and wanted to marry her. Waiting for the family heirloom to arrive. Waiting for a night like tonight. Now that it was here, he couldn't seem to hold his feelings in any longer.

"Here I am," she said. She shifted from one foot to the other then held out the glass of milk. "Your milk."

He looked at the glass then back to her face. She seemed as nervous as he was. Perhaps he had come on too strong. He needed to get in control of himself before he had her running for the top of the mountain.

"Thank you." He accepted the milk, though it was the last thing on his mind now. "Will your father be home soon? I have something very important to discuss with him."

A choked sort of laugh escaped her. "You don't really want to talk about important matters today."

Yes. Yes, he did.

"I mean, after all, it's Christmas Eve," she continued. "Time to celebrate our Lord's birth."

As far as Harlan was concerned, it was a perfect day to confess his love for the beautiful woman before him. Yet what if her pastor father thought differently of the matter?

He would have to see how her father felt about such things. Harlan nodded to himself. That was what he would do, sort of test the waters, see how her father responded before he dove into the proposal.

"Do you suppose he'll be home soon?" Harlan couldn't stop the shift in his stance. He had to do something to keep on his feet. He couldn't ruin this proposal now.

"I hope not," she muttered.

At least that was what he *thought* she said. "I beg your pardon?"

"I'm sure he will." She flashed him a sweet smile. He must have been mistaken.

"Good." Harlan set the milk on the side table and captured her hands in his own. He simply had to touch her. If he had to wait until her father got home to ask permission to marry her, the least he should be allowed was to rub his thumbs across her smooth skin. "I'm glad."

Something flashed in her eyes, something that looked suspiciously like. . .*panic*? She turned as if listening to something coming from the kitchen. "What was that, Grace?" she called.

He hadn't heard anything.

She turned back to him, her mouth twisted in apology. "I just need to go help Grace. . .in the kitchen. . . with dinner." She backed away from him until he had no choice but to release her. "In the kitchen." She turned on her heel and fled into the other room.

What was wrong with her?

"Good evening, Harlan."

He whirled around as Maddie's sister swept through the door that led into the hallway. "But I thought you were. . ." He trailed off as he gestured behind him toward the kitchen door.

"Thought I was what?" she asked.

He shook his head. "Forgive me," he said. "Good evening, Grace."

She smiled at him prettily.

How could sisters be two short years apart in age yet be so different in every way? Grace had hair like warm honey and pale green eyes the color of the jade statue he'd once seen on a trip to Philadelphia. Maddie's chocolate-colored hair made her meadow-green eyes shine and captured his heart like none other. God had sprinkled sweet freckles across her nose, like a fine dusting of cinnamon. Sugar and spice, they said.

"Sit, sit." Grace waved a hand toward the chair he'd recently abandoned.

He had no desire to perch his large frame on the tiny chair. It made him feel clumsy and unworthy. He needed all the confidence he could get tonight. "I think I'll just stand." He pulled on his lapels then lightly touched the box in his pocket once again.

Lord, please let her say yes. Let her father agree. Let this happen. Amen.

"Did you enjoy the cookies?" Grace asked.

"The best I ever ate."

Her eyes darkened until they were almost the color of her sister's. "I hope you didn't eat so many you spoiled your supper."

"Oh no," he assured her. "I'm really looking forward to the meal." And afterward.

"Well now, that's done." Maddie walked back into the room, smoothing her hands down her skirt.

"Wonderful." Grace rose to her feet and shot her sister a pointed look. "Perhaps now would be a good time for us to change for dinner. Before Father gets home."

Maddie smiled at Harlan apologetically. "Will you be okay here for a while, Harlan? We won't be long."

He dipped into a shallow bow. "Of course."

"Then excuse us, please." Grace moved toward her sister, linking arms as she guided Maddie toward the exit. "We'll be back as quickly as possible."

Harlan smiled. "Take your time. I have something I need to discuss with your father."

⁂

Maddie raced up the stairs, Grace mere steps behind her. "I've got to hurry," Maddie wheezed. Her father would never forgive her if she wasn't dressed properly when he arrived home for supper, and she would never be able to forgive herself if he arrived home before she got back downstairs. "I can't let Harlan talk to Pa."

"Right," Grace said, her own breathing heavy. "You go get your dress. I'll redo your hair. Then you can get back downstairs before Pa gets here."

Maddie nodded. "What about your hair?"

"I'll manage." She pushed Maddie into her room and followed behind her.

In record time, Maddie was dressed and on her way back down the stairs. She took them as fast as she dared, hating the way the bustle stuck out behind her like tail feathers. She wasn't at all sure about the fashion and would be grateful when it passed. But for now, the green and black velvet was her best dress and perfect for a Christmas Eve meal with her family. And Harlan.

She slowed her steps as she got to the bottom of the stairs, cautiously smoothing down her dress and running trembling fingers over her hair. Had she made it?

Her gaze flickered to the large front door. Father's hat hung on the coat tree just inside. She hadn't heard him come up the steps, which could only mean. . .

She spurred her feet into motion, running as fast and as ladylike as she possibly could as she rushed toward the parlor. She swung inside to find her father and Harlan shaking hands.

"Pa!" At her shrill summons, her father and Harlan both turned to stare at her. "I mean, good evening, Father. I trust you had a good evening?" He had spent the night at the small orphanage at the edge of town, doing his best to spread Christmas cheer to the children without family this holiday season.

"Why, yes, I was just telling Harlan here about one small lad."

Maddie nodded, trying to appear interested in what he had to say. Normally she would have been, but tonight. . . Well, she couldn't keep focused on such matters when she had messed things up like she had.

"And I was just telling your father that I had something very important to discuss with him." Harlan's eyes twinkled as if he were very pleased with himself.

Lord, what have I done? Please help me make this right.

Maddie's heart gave a painful thump, but she smiled through it all. "It's Christmas Eve. We can't discuss business on such a holiday."

"She's right, my boy." Her father clapped Harlan on the shoulder.

Much to her relief, Harlan returned the smile and gave a quick nod. "Whatever you say."

Perhaps the effect of the cookies was wearing off already. She could only pray that it was.

Then a look passed between the two men, and her hopes were dashed. Had she been too late getting to the parlor? Had Harlan already talked to her father about marriage?

She closed her eyes and said a quick prayer, hoping the Lord wasn't too confused at her change of heart. She had been praying for a proposal from Harlan for so long, it was more than strange to ask for anything different.

"Y'all come t' supper." Their housekeeper, Prissy, stuck her head through the kitchen door, her dark eyes gleaming. Prissy had been with them so long she was less like help and more like a member of the family.

Her father nodded. "As soon as Grace gets downstairs. What is keeping that girl?" He took his pocket watch from inside his waistcoat and checked the time.

"Here I am." Grace swept into the room with a gesture worthy of her name. And once again Maddie had a hard time feeling remorse for putting the love herbs in Harlan's cookies. Without a little help, Harlan would be like the rest of the men in Calico Falls and completely besotted with her beautiful sister.

She added shame and repentance to her growing prayer.

"Ah, good," their father said, holding out his arm to escort Grace to the table. What choice did Maddie have but to slip her own through Harlan's?

He was warm and strong, solid and kindly as he patted her hand where it lay in the bend of his elbow. But as they walked toward the dining room, his steps slowed until they were well behind the others.

"I spoke to your father a little," he whispered, bending low so only she could hear. He smelled of spice and sandalwood, and it took all of her willpower not to bury her nose in the folds of his suit and inhale his tangy scent.

"You w–what?" she stammered instead.

"I spoke to him a bit. Told him how much I have come to care for you."

"You—you have?"

"Oh yes." He flashed her a dazzling smile.

Why, oh why couldn't he smile at her like that without Old Lady Farley's help? Her heart melted despite the fact she knew his gesture to be untrue.

"I told him what a surprise I received finding love here."

What a surprise indeed.

"Will you do me a favor, Harlan?" She stilled her feet, needing a moment or two more before facing the rest of her family.

"Anything, my dear."

"Please don't say anything to him at supper. Let it be our little secret for a bit."

His blue eyes twinkled at the thought. "And that will make you happy?"

"Very much so," she lied.

"Then that is what we will do."

❦

He would never understand what lay in the chambers of a woman's heart.

He shot a quick look at her father, hoping Easton Sinclair understood his meaning. They had only talked a moment or two before Maddie had rushed back into the parlor. Long enough for Harlan to declare his love for the preacher's daughter, but not long enough to state his intentions. Yet Pastor Sinclair was a smart man; he'd figure it out in no time at all. Harlan could only hope the man would keep the news to himself and allow Maddie her time for a secret.

He pulled out a chair and seated her, then made his way around the table to the chair opposite hers. He wanted to see her pretty face as they dined. How wonderful it would be after they wed for him to look at her during every meal. The thought filled him with such joy, he felt heat rising in his face.

"I say," Pastor Sinclair said. "Are you all right, Harlan?"

Harlan choked back a smile then gave a discreet cough.

"It's gonna snow," Priscilla said, pushing through the kitchen door, the large plate of ham nearly hiding her face.

Harlan liked the sassy house worker. She had spunk and spirit, and it didn't hurt any that she had saved him from having to answer the uncomfortable question.

"What makes you say that?" Grace unfolded her napkin and placed it daintily on her lap.

"My rheumatism is actin' up somethin' terrible." Prissy set the platter on the table and slid into her place opposite Grace.

"Bow your heads," Pastor Sinclair instructed, bracing his elbows on the table. "Father Lord, we come to You tonight to ask thanks for this meal we are about to receive. Make our hearts grateful and our minds open to receive the nourishment as we sup and fellowship on this fine Christmas Eve. Thank You, Father, for our beautiful and growing family."

Something touched Harlan's leg, and he opened his eyes a bit to look across the table. If it was Maddie, he couldn't tell it. Her hands were clasped together so tightly that her knuckles were white and her eyes were squinted shut.

He closed his eyes again, sure he was mistaken.

"Father God, we ask that you bless this food, this day, and the wonderful souls sharing it."

There it was again.

He peeked a second time, his eyes centering on Grace. She caught his attention, nodding her head toward Maddie and then their father. She raised her brows in question.

Was she asking if he was going to talk to their father tonight? And here he thought he'd concealed his feelings for Maddie. He hadn't wanted to get either of their hopes up. After all, Calico Falls wasn't a large town, and he surely wouldn't be able to support her if he couldn't make his law practice survive. Thankfully his business had thrived, and he was prepared to ask for her hand.

He gave a small nod to Grace and closed his eyes again, but not before a look of panic shot across her face. What was wrong with her?

"Amen," the reverend said.

Everyone raised their heads and started passing around the platters and bowls of delicious potatoes, beans, ham, and cornbread.

It had been a long time since Harlan had had a home-cooked meal such as this, and he enjoyed every bite.

"I see the gingerbread cookies didn't spole yur appetite none."

At Prissy's observation, Maddie's father raised his head. "Cookies?"

Harlan swallowed and cleared his throat. "Yes sir. Maddie made me a batch of gingerbread cookies this afternoon. They were delicious."

"That sounds like a fine dessert." The reverend patted his stomach.

"I apologize." Harlan coughed. "But I believe I ate them all, sir."

"I had a few of 'em myself, and they were mighty tasty." Prissy scooped up a bite of potatoes and savored it as if reliving the spicy cookie all over again.

"There might have been a few more." Maddie ducked her head over her plate.

"Just like the ones I ate?" Harlan asked.

"No, thank goodness," Grace said.

"Um, actually, yes," Maddie quietly countered, looking at Grace helplessly.

"They were delicious," Harlan repeated, and smiled to show his appreciation.

Grace pushed her chair under the table, staring down her nose at each of them in turn. "I'm sure my sister can find us something else to eat for dessert." Her words seemed to challenge anyone to say differently.

"But the cookies were so delicious," Harlan said. "Life changing." He resisted the urge to wink at Maddie.

Grace shook her head. "You have no idea."

⁂

"Maddie, can I see you in the kitchen, please." Grace's words didn't quite form a request. In fact, her tone was closer to "Get in here now."

Maddie rose to her feet. "Excuse me," she said, nodding to the others in turn. Perhaps if she took off through the front door, Grace wouldn't chase her. After all, they were wearing their best dresses, and Grace had always been more of a lady than Maddie. Just like their mother, Pa always said.

Thinking better of it, she trudged behind her sister into the kitchen.

"Madeline Joy." Grace whirled on her the minute they were out of earshot of the others. "I thought you said the other cookies were. . .were. . ." She sputtered.

"Unaltered?" Maddie supplied.

Grace propped her hands on her hips. "Well?"

"I may have stretched the truth on that statement a bit."

"You lied."

Well, she wouldn't have put it like that. "I wasn't sure how much I should put in—"

"You bought a love potion from the crazy woman at the end of the lane and you didn't ask how much to use?" Grace's voice rose.

"Shh." Maddie glanced behind them, but thankfully no one burst in from the other room demanding to know the truth. "First of all, I didn't buy it, I bartered." And a right good trade she'd made, at that. Her second best dress for the entire bag of herbs.

Grace didn't look impressed with the fine details of the transaction.

"And it's not a love potion, just some herbs to make Harlan a little more. . .amicable toward marriage." What else was she supposed to do? It wasn't like he loved another or had stated his intentions toward someone else. He worked hard and steady, barely taking off time to go to church. Someone had to save him from himself.

"Do you honestly believe that?" Grace asked, her stance wilting just a bit.

"Oh Grace, he's so handsome and wonderful and handsome."

"So you've said."

"I really didn't mean any harm."

"I believe we've had this conversation already."

"What am I supposed to do?" She only wanted his love. She hadn't meant to ruin it all.

"Find some cake." Grace frowned. "And don't leave him alone with Pa."

∞

Maddie pasted on a smile and backed through the swinging door from the kitchen. "Who wants cake?"

She didn't pay any attention to the answers. The gingerbread cookies were in the trash, buried under this morning's coffee grounds. She couldn't risk Harlan eating any more of them.

Grace came behind her bearing the freshly brewed coffee to end their meal.

"You girls are so sweet, bringin' in dessert like this." Prissy smiled at them, her teeth a flash of ivory in her mocha-colored skin. It might not be fashionable to allow a person of color to share a table with those who were not, but her father said they were all the Lord's children and the color of skin didn't make one bit of difference to him. Or Him.

"You take care of us all the time," Grace said smoothly. "It's only proper for us to show our gratitude when we can."

Maddie set the tray on the table, her gaze immediately drawn to Harlan. How could one man be so handsome and perfect? He loved the Lord and was successful and well learned. He was everything a poor preacher's daughter from Arkansas could ever hope for. And the Lord had sent him to her. She just knew it.

"How about we postpone this cake for a bit and go into the study for a quick smoke?" Her father pushed back from the table, his gaze trained on Harlan.

Grace shot Maddie a quick look. *Do something now,* it said.

Once the men got to the study, the women would be locked out for most of the evening. She'd have no way to intervene.

Oh, she wanted Harlan to ask for her hand in marriage, but not like this. What a moment of weakness, when she had succumbed to the urge to seek outside help in getting Harlan to love her in return.

Shame filled her. She hadn't trusted the Lord. He was all the "outside help" she needed.

"Harlan," she practically purred. Whose voice was that? She cleared her throat and tried not to sound so desperate. "Harlan, will you take me for a quick stroll? I suddenly feel the need for. . ."

"Fresh air," Grace supplied.

"Yes, that's it," Maddie agreed. "Fresh air would be wonderful."

Harlan seemed to hesitate, but thankfully the powder she had added to the cookies kicked in and took over. He wouldn't be able to deny her anything tonight. Tomorrow might be another story altogether. But she would deal with that problem then. "Of course." He stood and nodded toward her father.

"We can talk when you get back," Pa said.

Maddie took a fortifying breath. Not if she had anything to say in the matter.

Chapter 2

Only a small patch of stars shone in the night sky. Clouds covered the rest, giving hope to Prissy's promise of snow.

Maddie pulled the sides of her wool cape a little closer around her as she silently questioned the wisdom of a winter night's walk. Too bad it wasn't a fragrant June evening with birds chirping and cicadas buzzing in the heat. But she had to get Harlan out of the house before he could embarrass himself in front of her father.

"Are you warm enough?" Harlan asked. Concern colored his voice. "We can go back in, if you'd like."

"Oh no," Maddie gushed, her enthusiasm more than one person should have. She told herself to calm down and shot him a quick smile. "I want to walk all the way down to the church."

"That far?"

"Of course," she lied. Quickly asking God for forgiveness, she continued. "It's Christmas Eve, the perfect day to go to the church. Don't you agree?" At least this last part was the truth.

Harlan returned her smile and nearly took her breath away. "Perfect," he said.

She looped her arm through his, and together they started off through the small crop of trees that hid the preacher's house from the rest of Calico Falls.

"It's a beautiful night," Harlan said. His strong form moved a little closer to her. They were alone, and the action was most inappropriate, but it was cold and she relished the warmth of him drawing near. If only he was so close because he truly loved her and wanted to be by her side always. That was everything a girl could ask for. Instead. . .

"Harlan," she started as they continued their walk, "there's something I need to talk to you about." She couldn't stand the guilt any longer. So far she had tricked him into eating tainted cookies, rebuffed his sweet marriage proposal, and led him out in the cold to correct her own mistakes. These were not the actions of a woman in love, but of a desperate woman who needed to get back in control of herself before she ruined Christmas for everyone involved.

She only had a short time before she would be able to send Harlan home for the evening, but she had to confess the truth before it ate up her insides.

"Yes, my love?"

Her heart tripped at the endearment, and her feet followed suit.

"Whoa, there." Harlan wrapped his arms around her. His embrace steadied her steps and kept her from falling face first into the packed dirt street of Calico Falls. But it had done more than that. It brought them close. So close. With only mere inches separating them. Inches that could be closed in a heartbeat.

Maddie inhaled, the action only bringing them closer, their frosted breath mingling in the night air.

They had come through the trees and into town, the church steeple just visible at the end of the way.

The sight of the cross standing straight and tall against the dark, clouded sky gave her bravery she hadn't had before.

She wedged her hands between herself and Harlan, putting some distance between them and successfully ending the potential kiss that hung around them.

"I must tell you something," she breathed, hating the words before she even said them. She prayed they wouldn't change how he felt about her forever. *Lord, please let him understand that everything I did, I did out of love.*

"I went to Old Lady Farley and got some. . .ground spices and herbs to put in the cookies."

He grinned. "They were delicious."

"Not those kinds of herbs." She bit her lip, trying to come up with the best explanation and falling short. "They were ones to make you fall in love with me."

To her surprise, he threw back his head and laughed long and loud into the cold night. "You are a jewel, Maddie Sinclair."

"But—" she started, sputtering to answer. This was not how she expected him to respond. Where was the indignation, the accusations, and hurt?

The poor man was so far gone he couldn't even believe the truth. Those herbs must have been more potent than she'd originally thought.

"Harlan, listen to me." She grabbed his arms, holding him still so he would face her. He had to understand how serious the matter was.

But instead of searching her face and seeing the truth, he tilted his head back and scanned the sky. "It's snowing."

Pure white crystal flakes drifted down from the clouds. They were close to the mountains, but not far enough up that they'd ever had a white Christmas that Maddie could recall. Watching the snow fall was like a miracle in itself.

"Come on." Harlan grabbed her hand, and together they raced toward the church.

Maddie couldn't stop the laugh from escaping her as they ran. The snow started to fall faster. By the time they reached the portico at the tiny white clapboard church, the ground was nearly covered.

Harlan released her hand as they stepped under the cover. He brushed the snow from his shoulders and gave her that heart-stopping smile. "I guess we should have run back toward your house."

"Most probably," Maddie said, but she wouldn't have missed the scene before her for anything. Snow fell around their sleepy little town. Candles twinkled in the windows of houses and shops alike. Pine wreaths hung on the doors, tied with red ribbon and strips of flour sacks. A hush hovered over the town, a quiet air of expectation. Tomorrow was Christmas. "It's beautiful," she whispered.

"Yes," he agreed, but he wasn't looking at the town. He was staring at her, that gleam back in his blue eyes.

"Harlan, what I said back there, I was serious."

He shook his head. "You think I asked to marry you because of something Old Lady Farley gave you?"

She solemnly nodded. At least now he was starting

to understand. As much as it hurt her, she was glad.

"Maddie Sinclair, you should know better."

"I know." She had to push the words past the lump in her throat.

"You of all people should know that she's a crazy old hen. Why, she probably gave you a mess of ground-up, dried grass and charged you, to boot."

"What? No, she gave me some love herbs, and I baked them into the cookies. Then you asked me to marry you." Couldn't he understand? How many times did she have to say it before he realized she was telling the truth?

"The cookies were delicious, I might add. But not enough to make me fall in love with you." He seemed to think about it a moment. "Well, maybe. They were pretty tasty."

"Harlan Calhoun. I need you to be serious. I did something terribly wrong. You have to believe me."

"Oh, I believe you." His eyes twinkled, taking all the validity from his words. And it surely didn't help when he dropped to one knee there on the portico and clasped her hands in his. "Maddie Sinclair, would you do me the pleasure of being my wife?"

Tears immediately sprang to her eyes. Her hands were in his warm ones, and she let the tears fall.

"Harlan." She nearly choked on the love and remorse clogging her throat. "I don't know what to say."

Oh, she knew what to say. She had to tell him no. As much as she loved him, as long as she had waited for this moment, she had to tell him no. And then pray like everything that he would still feel the same once the cookies lost their effect.

Not that she expected those prayers to be answered.

"You say yes," he gently explained. He released her hands to remove something from the inside pocket of his coat. A jewelry box.

Her heart pounded, and her mouth dried to ash as he lifted the lid. Nestled inside the carved box, atop a deep burgundy velvet cushion, was a cameo. It was beautiful and fragile and special. She wanted nothing more than to remove it and hold it close. Cherish it always.

"This was my grandmother's," he continued. "But I want you to have it as a symbol of my love for you."

"Oh Harlan." She clamped one hand over her mouth to keep from saying more. As badly as she wanted to declare her eternal love in return, this was wrong. "I can't accept this," she said, her choked sob escaping between her numb fingers.

His earnest smile never wavered. "Of course not.

You can't say yes without my talking to your father first. Please forgive my eagerness. But I have no patience where love is concerned."

If only that were true.

She bit her lip again, this time drawing blood as she struggled to keep words she couldn't say from escaping. "I think it's time we headed back."

The ground was completely white. Perhaps it was past time to go home, weather-wise at least. But when they got back to her house, he was sure to want to talk to her father, and that was something she simply couldn't allow.

She looked out at the falling snow. They couldn't stay here much longer without scandalizing the entire town. With a sigh, she pulled him to his feet. "We have to go back now," she said. She'd worry about the rest of it later.

His smile grew positively dazzling, brighter than the snow they had to trudge through to make it back to her house on the edge of town. "I'm glad to see you're so. . .enthusiastic."

"What?" He had completely misunderstood her intentions. "That's not what I meant. It's snowing harder. If we don't get back soon, we'll never make it."

Harlan tilted his head, his expression so lost and

perplexed she wanted to reach out and wipe it away with the tips of her fingers. "Are you saying you don't want to marry me?"

She opened her mouth to respond. His question had no right answer. If she said no, Harlan would forever think she didn't love him. If she said yes, then he would want to propose—for real, in front of her father and with his blessing—tonight. And what happened tomorrow when the cookies no longer had control of his emotions and his thinking was clear? How would he feel about being trapped into marriage with the preacher's plain daughter?

"Let's go," she said, turning toward the steps leading away from the church. It was best not to answer at all and say another prayer that the Lord would somehow see her through.

Yet a tiny voice inside whispered, *You got yourself into this. It's up to you to get yourself out of it.*

Maddie wasn't sure if it was the Lord or her own conscience. She suspected it might be a little of both.

Still, it wouldn't stop her from praying. And with a lot of blessing from above, she would somehow be able to stall Harlan until it was time for him to head back to his own house. Then, and only then, would she breathe a sigh of relief.

Harlan grabbed Maddie's hand, and together they dashed back through the snow. It was as if the heavens knew he needed an enchanted night to ask her to be his wife. And what was more magical than snow on Christmas Eve?

The earth glistening with the crystal flakes lent a surreal backdrop to the midnight-blue sky. It was almost Christmas, the most wondrous day of the year. Maddie Sinclair was about to agree to be his wife. And everything was perfect. He'd never felt so blessed.

Well, at least he thought she was going to agree to be his wife. But this nonsense about bewitched cookies. Ridiculous. He hoped her crazy notions about magical herbs weren't enough to keep her from saying yes.

Oh, the cookies were tasty indeed. But they weren't magical. And delicious as they were, they couldn't make him fall in love. Because he was already there. He had loved her from the first time he had seen her. She had been standing at her father's side, welcoming the congregation into their tiny church. Harlan was brand-new to town, the dust not even wiped from his shoes, but he knew he had to keep his covenant with the Lord. Despite his exhaustion and weariness from the trip west, he'd donned his best suit and walked to the church.

She had been wearing a dress as blue as the June sky, the color lending its hue to her green eyes to turn them the color of the ocean. Her deep brown hair had been pulled back with a bit of ivory lace that perfectly matched the trimmings on her dress. And in that instant, he had fallen completely in love.

He allowed his gaze to drift toward her now. She was even more beautiful, with the cold staining her cheeks a fetching pink and adding an extra sparkle to her eyes. And he loved her even more.

How silly and sweet that she had thought she could make him fall in love with her by using a crazy old woman's love potion. He couldn't love her any more than he already did. Well, that was his verdict today. Tomorrow might bring even more affection for the lovely woman at his side.

For her to go to such lengths to make him fall in love with her. . .well, that had to say something about her own feelings, didn't it?

She had yet to tell him how she felt. But she had to love him. She just had to.

They made it back to her house in record time, snowflakes clinging to their hair and clothes.

"Maddie. Harlan." Grace met them at the door, concern etched into every inch of her face. "We were so worried about you."

Maddie smiled at her sister, the action warming his heart from the inside out. "It's snowing, Grace. It's a Christmas miracle. That has to mean something, right?"

Grace shook her head. "Maddie, you didn't. . ." Her words trailed off as she helped her sister out of her wet cloak. She brushed the last of the snowflakes from Maddie's hair as Maddie whispered, "He asked me to marry him."

"What did you say?" Grace returned in the same whisper.

Harlan took off his coat but held it in his arms, waiting for the two of them to finish.

"What could I say? I told him we had to talk to Pa."

"Oh Maddie."

"You didn't tell Pa, right? Please, Gracie, you can't tell Pa."

"What are we supposed to do?"

Maddie shook her dark head. "I don't know, but please don't tell him. He'll never understand."

"I won't tell him," Harlan said.

The sisters turned to him as if they had just remembered he was there.

"Harlan," Grace greeted, her voice overloud in the small entryway. "Let's get you into the parlor where there's a fire going." She took his coat and hung it on the rack next to Maddie's.

"Is your father in there?" he asked as Grace led him down the hall.

"He's in the study having a smoke." She wrinkled her nose as if this was the absolute worst thing. Harlan didn't partake of tobacco often. He knew it was the vogue thing in all the best houses in the East, but he'd never developed a taste for it. Still, he would much rather be in the study not having a smoke with her father than in the parlor alone. How was he supposed to ask for Maddie's hand half a house away from the blessing he needed?

He started to protest, but Grace seemed deaf as she led him toward the parlor.

"Now you wait here, and I'll be back shortly with some hot cocoa to help warm you up."

"You don't happen to have any more of those cookies I had earlier?"

Grace's emerald eyes grew wide and her cheeks turned pale. "No," she said, her voice sounding much like a mother's to a child asking for candy. "No more cookies for you." She disappeared through the door leading back into the kitchen.

Her expression was perplexing to be sure. It was

almost as if she, too, believed that Maddie had made him fall in love with her.

He had to put a stop to this nonsense. If he couldn't ask for Maddie's hand before he had to leave for the night—

He shook his head. He'd had it planned out perfectly in his mind. A Christmas Eve proposal, a kiss under the mistletoe, a spring wedding.

His fingers slipped into his coat pocket, touching the box containing his grandmother's cameo. He had imagined it pinned to the ivory lace of Maddie's wedding dress, nestled at her throat, showing the world that she was his.

"There you are, my boy." Easton Sinclair swept into the room, bringing with him the smoky tang of tobacco. "Seems Prissy was right." He nodded toward the window where the fat white flakes continued to fall.

"Yes sir." Harlan cleared his throat, his prepared speech deserting him in his time of need.

"Get over here closer to the fire before you catch your death of cold," the reverend instructed. His voice was deep and booming even when he wasn't in the pulpit, and Harlan found himself immediately complying.

The crackling fire warmed him. He hadn't realized he was chilled. He was still floating on the warmth of Maddie's sweet smile.

"You said you had some business to discuss with me, young man." That was just like Pastor Sinclair, straight to the point.

"Not business, really. More of a personal matter." He opened his mouth to continue but was interrupted.

"Here we are." Grace pushed her way back into the parlor, a tray of treats balanced in her arms.

"Ah, something to warm us on the inside." Pastor Sinclair nodded happily.

Asking for Maddie's hand would have to wait for a few more minutes. Her father, it seemed, had something of a sweet tooth. But Harlan could wait a little longer. Despite her wild claim that she had made him fall in love with her, he knew the truth.

Ever the gracious hostess, Grace poured cups of steaming cocoa and passed out the tea biscuits shaped like Christmas trees.

"Too bad there aren't any more of those gingerbread cookies," Pastor Sinclair said.

"Too bad," Grace murmured.

Harlan was amazed that a sensible woman like Grace Sinclair would fall for such nonsense, but there it was. "Speaking of the cookies. . ."

Grace shook her head. "You promised."

"Promised what?" Pastor Sinclair asked.

"Did everyone forget I was in the house?" Maddie picked that very moment to sweep back into the room. As usual, she stole the breath from Harlan's lungs.

"Maddie, thank goodness." Grace hustled to her sister's side, whispering in her ear with an urgent hiss.

Harlan couldn't make out the words, but the intention was clear.

Maddie's eyes widened, and she gave a stiff nod.

"Girls." It seemed the reverend was accustomed to his daughters sharing secrets and thought the custom rude.

"Forgive me, Pa." Grace bowed toward him but offered no explanation.

"Since we are all here—and this seems to be turning into a family matter—I have something I need to discuss with you, Pastor Sinclair."

Maddie started coughing, choking really, though on what, Harlan could not determine. She'd had nothing to eat, nothing to drink.

Once again Grace raced to her side, patting her solicitously on the back and helping her over to the settee as she continued to cough and hiccup. "Let me get you something to drink, sister."

Maddie nodded as another fit of whatever ailed her

came upon her again. This one though seemed a little less genuine than the one before.

Harlan immediately regretted his assumption. Maddie was clearly in distress as she covered her mouth with an embroidered handkerchief, tears welling in her eyes.

"There, there," Grace crooned as she poured Maddie a cup of cocoa. "I hope that cold isn't already setting in. You'll catch your death being out on a night like this."

"A warm drink will spruce her right up." Pastor Sinclair nodded toward his daughters then turned to face Harlan. "You were saying?"

"Well sir, I—"

Maddie jumped to her feet, her recovery miraculous indeed. "Harlan Calhoun, you can't stay a minute longer. You'll never be able to get home in this storm if you do."

Grace rushed from the room before he could reply, returning in mere seconds with his coat draped over one arm and his hat in her hand. "Prissy dried your coat by the fire, so you are ready to go. So glad you could join us this evening." She held his coat out to him. When he didn't immediately take it, she shook it at him.

"Would someone like to tell me what's going on in this house tonight?" Pastor Sinclair's booming words were less of a question and more of a "someone had better start explaining" command.

"Nothing, Father." Grace and Maddie murmured their reply in unison, but neither one met their father's piercing gaze.

"Mr. Calhoun will not be going anywhere in this weather." His tone brooked no argument.

It didn't deter Maddie. "But—"

She stopped as Grace elbowed her. "Perhaps we should play a Christmas game."

"Like charades."

Their father blustered. "Perhaps we should read from the Bible instead."

"Wonderful idea." Harlan rubbed his hands together. He loved reading from the book of Luke the details of the birth of their Lord and Savior. What a perfect way to spend Christmas Eve. Reading God's word with the woman he loved and her family.

Maddie bustled off to find Prissy so she could join the festivities, while Grace continued to pin him with a warning stare.

Harlan glanced toward the preacher and tried to relax. He was anxious to state his intentions. To gain her father's blessing, to give Maddie the cameo, to start the rest of their life together on this special day. Yet it seemed all that would have to wait. But only for a while. He wanted to make Maddie his wife. And he would. As soon as he convinced her the herbs she got from Old Lady Farley were nothing more than a hoax.

∞

"Why don't you start off, Harlan?" Pa looked to their guest and handed him the Bible.

Maddie closed her eyes as he read, his deep voice like velvet as he shared with them the story of Mary and Joseph. Of their travels to Bethlehem, of no room at the inn. Of having a child and laying the babe in a manger.

When he finished reading, Maddie was certain she had never loved him more. Why, oh why had she felt it necessary to taint the cookies? Why hadn't she left it up to the Lord? And how was she supposed to know when the effects were worn off? When he no longer wanted to marry her? It was heartbreaking. The herbs could last two hours or two weeks! How was she supposed to know?

And now he was staying the night.

"Maddie?"

She glanced up for the first time since they had

gathered in the parlor. The two of them were alone. "Where did everyone go?" She had been daydreaming so much she hadn't heard the others leave.

"Your father went back to his study. Prissy said she was turning in for the night, and Grace went to find me a stocking to hang on the mantel."

"She did?"

"I told her it wasn't necessary, but. . ." He trailed off. Not that he had to say more. She knew how determined her sister could be when she set her mind to something. If Grace wanted Harlan to have a Christmas stocking, then a Christmas stocking he would have.

"At least you won't be getting coal in yours." Maddie spoke the words before thinking then clamped her hand over her mouth. "That was churlish. I'm sorry."

He smiled at her, his face lighting up with love. What she wouldn't give to have him look at her like that for now and always. Without the tricks of Old Lady Farley. "You're not going to get coal in your stocking," he said. "That I can promise you. By some chance you do, I think I know a gift that will more than make up for it." He touched his chest, close to his heart. The exact spot where she knew he had stored the beautiful cameo he'd presented her earlier.

"Speaking of," he started. He stood and stretched. With a smile, he pulled on the legs of his brown pants, and the snowy-white shirt sleeves that peeked out from under his suit coat. "I have something important to discuss with your father."

"No!" Maddie tugged him back to the settee next to her. The surprise attack was most probably what pulled him off his feet, but she would take any help she could get. "Harlan, you can't."

"Of course I can." His smile was infectious, sweet and pure.

"But you promised."

A frown pulled at his forehead, and he pushed to his feet. "I did not."

"You did," she protested. "You promised me and Grace that you wouldn't say anything to Pa about the cookies."

To her surprise, he threw back his head and laughed. "I'm not telling him about the cookies. I'm going to ask for your hand in marriage."

She pulled him back down next to her. "That's the same thing."

"It is not." He was on his feet in an instant.

Maddie jerked on his arm until he agreed to sit once more. "It is."

He shook his head, but thankfully he didn't try to get away. "Is this about the herbs again?"

"That's all it's been about."

"Maddie, you're being ridiculous. There was nothing wrong with those cookies."

"Oh Harlan, I wish you were right."

"I am right." He took her hands, his blue eyes searching hers. "I want to make you my wife. And I want us to be wed this spring when the dogwoods and the daffodils are in bloom. It's not so much to ask."

"No," she whispered, caught in the warm cocoon of his voice.

He leaned toward her, and she caught the scent of his sandalwood aftershave and the spice that had seemed to follow him all night. "You will be a beautiful bride," he whispered, drawing closer still.

"You think I'm beautiful?" she asked, the words barely a whisper in the waning distance between them.

"More than you will ever know." His words washed over her, his warm breath sweet with the scent of chocolate. His gaze flickered to her lips.

He was going to kiss her!

Maddie jumped to her feet.

Harlan pulled her back down beside him. "Where are you going?"

"Uh, to help Grace find you a stocking." She was back on her feet in an instant.

"I don't need a stocking." He tugged her back down beside him. Was he even closer now?

"Of course you do." She hopped to her feet for only a heartbeat before he pulled her back down.

"Stop it, Maddie. You're making me dizzy."

She pressed a hand to her forehead. He wasn't the only one. "You can't kiss me, Harlan." Now those were words she never thought she'd say.

"You're right, of course. I shouldn't be so forward until after I've spoken to your father."

He rose to his feet, and she pulled him back down.

"Oh no," he said. "We're not going to start this again."

She laid a hand on his arm, effectively stilling him beside her. "Please, Harlan."

"Please what, Maddie? I'll do anything for you."

"Then don't ask my father for my hand." She almost choked on the words. "At least, not until the cookies—" She shook her head, unable to finish. "I'm not sure you'll want to then, but wait. . .for me."

His gaze bored into hers. "It means that much to you?"

She nodded. Couldn't he see this was for his own good?

"Then I'll wait. But only until the morning. And not because I believe in some cookie mumbo-jumbo. But because you asked me to."

That was good enough for her. "Thank you," she whispered, her heart breaking.

Lord, dear Lord, please let him still love me in the morning.

Chapter 3

Christmas morning dawned bright and sunny, the warm rays bouncing off the blinding white snow. Maddie threw back the covers and rushed to get dressed, more excited than she had ever been on the Lord's birthday.

She said a quick prayer, since her joy had less to do with God and everything to do with Harlan Calhoun. Maybe today she would know the truth.

A knock sounded on the door, and Grace quickly slipped into Maddie's room. "Are you ready?"

Maddie patted her hair in place. "Almost." She couldn't stop the smile of excitement racing across her face. She clasped her brush to her breast and turned to face her sister. "Today's the day. Oh Grace. I prayed and prayed last night. Do you think Harlan will still love me today?"

The frown that pulled at her sister's brow was anything but reassuring. "How are you supposed to know, Maddie?"

Maddie dropped the brush on her dressing table and whirled around to face her sister. "I—I—" she sputtered. "I guess I'll just know." But her words sounded small in the space between them.

"Did you 'just know' yesterday?"

Maddie buried her face in her hands, her excitement draining away like rain off the roof. "What am I going to do?"

Grace hugged her close. "As I see it, you can get down there and tell Pa all about what happened, or you can go keep the two of them apart for a while longer."

Maddie straightened, wiping the tears from her cheeks as a new determination filled her. "That's what I'll do. I'll make him take me for a walk—"

"Another one?"

"—and keep him and Pa apart until it's safe for him to go home."

"Have you seen the snow out there? He may be here for days."

"Then I'll pray for the snow to melt. Pray with me, Grace."

Her sister shook her head. "I'll pray all right, for you to return to your senses."

Maddie stuck out her tongue at Grace like she had when they were children. "I have my senses. Just pray that Harlan comes back to his."

And with that she raised the hem of her skirt and rushed out the door. Her plan would be for naught if Harlan got to her father first.

She skipped down the stairs as fast as she dared, saying a little prayer with each step that her father had somehow managed to sleep in and wasn't already—

"Merry Christmas, Madeline." Her father beamed at her from his place by the mantel. The stockings had already been filled with crunchy nuts and delicious oranges. At least she hoped that was what caused the rounded bulges in her sock and not coal.

"Merry Christmas, Maddie."

She whirled around to see Harlan casually standing by the big armchair next to the Christmas tree. He must have been sitting there the entire time, standing when she entered the room. She was too late.

"Have you been awake long?" she asked, looking from one man to the other.

"Oh, a while." Harlan's eyes twinkled as he spoke. If the look on his face was any indication, then he had been up long enough to talk to her father.

"Harlan here was just telling me about the latest fad on the East Coast."

"He was?" Did that mean he hadn't been asking for

her hand? Maybe she wasn't too late after all.

"Are you ready to hear this?" her father asked with a chuckle. "Wedding cakes."

Maddie stumbled but managed to catch herself before she fell headlong onto the rug. "Wedding cakes?" she whispered, her hopes falling like last night's snow.

"It seems the bride gets this large cake all elaborately decorated with fruit and flowers. It sounds like quite a sight."

Maddie turned toward Harlan, the question she so desperately needed to ask stuck somewhere between her brain and her lips.

"It's morning, Maddie," he said, as if he could read her thoughts.

"It is," she agreed, carefully forming her words. She wanted nothing less than to jump up and down and scream in frustration. Instead, she spoke as calmly as possible. "Harlan, will you take a walk with me before breakfast?"

"Why, Daughter, it's below freezing out there."

"Please, Harlan."

He gave a quick nod. "Get your coat, my dear."

Thankfully, her father didn't protest further. Maddie donned her cloak and hustled Harlan out the door as quickly as possible.

The air wasn't quite as cold as it had been the night before, but still their breaths came out in little puffs of vapor.

"It's a beautiful day." Harlan looked up at the cloudless Christmas sky, squinting against the bright rays of the sun.

"How are you. . .feeling this morning?"

She hated Grace's logic. How was she supposed to know if Harlan was over the cookies? Maybe she should run down to Old Lady Farley's and ask.

Maddie pushed the thought away. That was no way to keep her little secret.

"I slept like a baby," Harlan replied, stepping off the porch and into the pile of snow lining the house.

"Any. . .changes this morning?"

He turned back to face her. "Is that what this is all about?"

"What?" she asked with feigned innocence. She had to know. And how would she find out without asking?

"Is this about those cookies?" He shook his head. "I was hoping you would be over it by this morning."

Me, too. "I can't believe you aren't taking this more seriously." She stamped her foot on the porch for emphasis. A small avalanche of snow fell from the roof, loosened by her motion.

"Whoa!" Harlan danced backward, but not before the snow cascaded around him. He shuffled a bit more as he tried to shake off the snow.

"Harlan!" Maddie raced off the porch. "Are you all right?" She slipped on the last step and fell headlong into his arms.

He took a step back, and another, trying to regain his balance; then the two of them fell into the snow.

The breath was knocked out of her as she fell, landing atop Harlan with a thud. It took a moment for her to regain her composure, a minute of listening to his heart beat under her ear and his own labored breathing as he caught his wind again.

"Oh!" Maddie pushed herself away and struggled to stand. Harlan managed the feat before her, reaching out a hand to help pull her upright.

"See where all this nonsense has gotten us?" He smiled as he brushed the snow from his clothes.

Tears rose in Maddie's eyes. "It's not nonsense. And what I did was wrong. Can't you see that? I'm trying to make amends, but you just won't listen." Her words ended on a strangled sob.

"Shh. . .shh. . ." Harlan pulled her to him, holding her close and rubbing a hand down her back. "Maddie Sinclair, despite your intentions and all your harebrained ideas about these cookies, I came here in love with you, and today when I leave, I will still be in love with you."

"And tomorrow?" she asked, pulling away so she could see his face.

"Still in love." He smiled.

Oh how she loved his smile. And oh how she wanted to believe what he said was true. "But—"

He shook his head. "What do I have to do to make you understand? I sent for the cameo. I came to ask for your hand. Can't you see that whatever you got from Old Lady Farley was just a ruse to take your money?"

"I bartered," Maddie started then broke off at Harlan's stern look. "I don't know," she whispered, wishing she had the answer. She wanted to believe him. She truly did, but the nagging doubts and Grace's voice of reason won out.

"I tell you what. Let's go get some of those flapjacks Prissy promised me last night, and maybe this whole thing will work itself out."

"Maybe," she murmured as he released her. She looped her arm through his and allowed him to lead her back into the house.

❧

Harlan stepped into the warmth of the house, his mind going at full speed. How was he ever going to convince his headstrong and silly Maddie that she had been taken by the "lady" who lived at the end of the lane? Old Lady Farley was a trickster, to be sure. He had no doubt that Maddie believed that she had done something wrong. Her tears of remorse were more than enough proof of that. And even a family heirloom couldn't convince her otherwise.

"Can you two not stay out of the snow?" Grace bustled into the entryway, a towel at the ready.

Harlan looked down to see he was already standing in a puddle of melted snow. "I'm sorry," he said sheepishly. "Forgive me, I fell."

"Of course." Grace smiled at him as he lifted his feet to stand on the towel and then helped Maddie take off her cloak.

Grace took it from him, and he removed his own coat.

"I'll have Prissy hang these by the fire just as soon as breakfast is finished."

"Is that what I smell?" Maddie asked.

The entire foyer was filled with the delicious scent of vanilla and nutmeg.

"Prissy's flapjacks."

"Smells delicious," Harlan said. And a bit familiar.

"Well, dry off and meet us at the table," Grace said.

"Prissy is setting it now." She started toward the kitchen then stopped and turned back to face them. "And there's no time to take advantage of. . .ahem." She pointed to a spot above their heads.

Harlan looked up at the sprig of mistletoe hanging from the ceiling. Why had he never noticed that before?

Grace smiled and pushed through the door that led to the kitchen.

Harlan looked to Maddie.

She swallowed hard as she returned his stare.

He took a step toward her.

"Harlan, I—"

But he wasn't about to take no for an answer. She loved him, and despite all her crazy ideas about love herbs and cookies, he loved her, too.

He took her by the arms and pulled her close—not close enough that their bodies touched, but still near enough he could breathe in the lilac scent of her soap and the crisp smell of outdoors.

She seemed about to protest, but her eyes fluttered closed a second before he lowered his head and pressed his lips to hers.

Her lips were soft, sweet beneath his, and he couldn't wait until she agreed to be his bride.

She sighed as he lifted his head. Her eyes opened and stared into his.

"Do you believe me now?"

She pulled away, pressing the back of one hand against her lips. "Harlan, I—"

"What, Maddie?" The game was growing tiresome, but he wouldn't give up. He *couldn't* give up.

"I want to believe you," she said. "I really do."

"Do you love me, Maddie?" He had to hear her say it one more time.

"I do," she whispered.

"Then I won't give up. I won't bother you again today. But I'll be here every day after until you realize that my love for you is genuine."

Without waiting for her response, he turned and made his way to the dining room.

⌘

Maddie watched him go, the warmth of his lips pressed against hers still tingling. She had wanted to melt into his embrace, like the snow they tracked in from outside. But she held herself in check.

He would be here every day? For how long? One week? Two? Or would he walk out of her life this afternoon, never to return?

"Maddie," Grace called from the other room. "We're waiting on you."

She hustled into the dining room to find everyone already seated. Once again she sat across from Harlan. Her cheeks filled with heat as she recalled their kiss under the mistletoe. But he looked at her like she was almost a stranger. Had the cookies finally worn off? The thought made her heart ache in her chest.

"Let's pray," her father said.

Maddie bowed her head as her father thanked the Lord for the beautiful day, the wonderful company, nourishing food, and His Son who had died for them all. She silently added an entreaty for forgiveness for her transgressions and a plea that one day Harlan would forgive her as well.

"Amen," Pa concluded.

Everyone raised their heads, and the platters of food were passed around. There were stacks of sweet-smelling flapjacks with fresh butter and rich maple syrup, bowls of fried potatoes, and mounds of country ham to be shared.

Everything tasted so delicious, Maddie was soon reaching for another couple of flapjacks to complete her meal. They were just so good.

"Prissy, I say you have outdone yourself this morning."

Their housekeeper smiled at the pastor's praise. "Thank ye, suh. I put in those special spices you left fur me."

Maddie's fork slipped from her fingers and clattered onto the table.

Harlan stopped eating, his fork suspended midway between his plate and his mouth.

Grace coughed delicately into her napkin.

Only Prissy and their father seemed oblivious to the strain at the table.

"What did you say?" Maddie asked, recovering as quickly as she could. Maybe she'd misunderstood. Maybe her father really did bring their housekeeper a bag of spices from the general store. Surely Prissy hadn't found the bag Maddie had gotten from Old Lady Farley. After all, Maddie had thrown that away herself. Hadn't she?

With all the confusion yesterday over the cookies and Harlan's impulsive proposal, Maddie couldn't remember. But surely she wouldn't have been so careless with something so important.

"Why, I found a bag of spices in the kitchen yesterdee. I put 'em in the flapjacks. They came out good, huh?"

"Very tasty," Pa agreed. "But I didn't leave you any spices. Though after tasting these flapjacks, I may have to remember to do so in the future."

Maddie's heart sank. "This bag," she started, "was it

small and made out of a scrap of flour sack?"

"Why yes it was," Prissy answered.

"And was it tied with a small leather string?"

"Yes'um." Prissy continued to eat, not realizing the tragedy of what she had done.

"How could you have been so careless?" Grace hissed.

Maddie kicked her under the table.

Grace shot her a look and rose. "I apologize for interrupting our meal, but Maddie, can I see you in the kitchen." It wasn't a question.

Maddie shook her head.

"May we be excused, Pa?" Grace turned her attention to their father, and Maddie settled down in her seat a bit more.

Christmas must have put him in a good mood, or maybe it was the tainted flapjacks, but their father nodded his consent.

"But—" Maddie tried to protest, but Grace hauled her to her feet despite her sputters and dragged her toward the kitchen.

Just before they pushed through the swinging door, Maddie heard Harlan say, "If you would excuse me, too, sir?"

Grace turned on her the minute they were alone.

"What have you done?"

"What have *I* done?" she protested.

They weren't alone for long. Harlan pushed his way inside. "Is she talking about what I think she's talking about?"

Maddie nodded and bit her lip.

"I told you this would come to no good," Grace scolded.

"I can't believe the two of you actually believe all this nonsense." Harlan shook his head.

"Oh, we believe it all right." Grace propped her hands on her hips and shot Maddie a look.

"What?" she asked. Then her defenses crumbled, and she wilted like a pansy in August. "I'm sorry." She ducked her head and sniffed. "I never meant for any of this to happen."

"Maddie." Harlan's voice was firm and commanding. "Is this what you put in the cookies?"

She looked up to find him holding the bag she had gotten from Old Lady Farley. She nodded miserably.

He lifted it to his nose and sniffed.

"Harlan, no." Maddie rushed over to him and pulled the bag from his grasp. "Don't do that. You might ingest more of it."

He chuckled. "Maddie, when are you going to believe me?"

How could she?

He tossed the bag on the counter. "If whatever it was she gave you was supposed to make me fall in love with you, then why aren't we all in love with everyone sitting at the table? We all ate it this morning."

"Maybe it has a delayed effect." It was the best reason Maddie could come up with, and it sounded weak even to her own ears.

Grace eased open the door just a crack, only enough that she could peek at their father and Prissy still seated at the table.

"What's happening out there?" Maddie asked.

"They're drinking coffee," Grace whispered in return.

"And that's it?"

Grace jerked away from the door. It closed with a swoosh. "I think they saw me."

"He wasn't proposing or anything?"

Grace shook her head.

"See?" Harlan said. "If they both ate the herbs— and we know they did—then they should be falling in love with each other."

Hope burst through Maddie. What he was saying was logical, and yet she was afraid to let herself believe. If what he said was true, then he could really and truly love her. But she could only allow herself to believe that when she was absolutely certain. Otherwise she would end up heartbroken and alone.

"What is going on in here?"

Grace jumped back as Pa burst through the kitchen door, missing her by mere inches.

"Pa," Maddie gasped.

Grace pressed one hand to her breast, and Harlan tried not to laugh.

Maddie shot him a look. This was not funny.

"I'm waiting."

"Well," Grace started, obviously trying to stall but not sure what she should say. That was Grace, ever truthful. Maddie was surprised her sister had kept the secret this long.

"It's okay, Grace." It was time for her to step up and tell the truth. No matter the consequences. "It's my fault." The tension that had been in Maddie's shoulders suddenly loosened, and she knew this was the right thing to do. Well, she had known it all along, but there was a comfort in the telling. "I went to Old Lady Farley and bought some herbs day before yesterday."

"Her name is Eunice Farley, and you will refer to her as Miss Farley."

"Yes, Pa."

"Why did you go buy herbs at her house?" To her

father's credit, he didn't so much as falter when he said the word *house* to refer to the pitiful shack that squatted at the edge of town.

"I wanted to make Harlan fall in love with me." She ducked her head as she said the words, ashamed to admit them aloud and to her pious father. What an embarrassment she had to be to him.

"And you thought Eunice Farley could help you with that?"

She nodded as shame washed over her.

To her surprise, her father laughed. "Are you saying that Eunice Farley sold you a love potion?"

"It wasn't a potion exactly. Just a bag of herbs." She was dodging the issue, but she couldn't seem to keep the words from slipping out.

"The same bag of herbs that Prissy added to our breakfast cakes this morning?"

"The very one." Harlan came to stand by her, and Maddie was immediately bolstered by his presence.

Pa shook his head. "I hope you learned your lesson."

Maddie hated when her father used that tone. That "you should know better, I thought I raised you better than this, what would your mother have to say about this?" tone he got at times like these.

"I'm sorry, Pa, I just. . ." She struggled to finish.

"You didn't trust the Lord to provide."

"No," she said, her voice small.

"Come." Her father motioned for her to follow him. "Let's go talk about this in the parlor. You, too, Harlan. It seems this concerns you as well."

∞

The last thing Maddie wanted to do was have her father berate her reckless behavior. She deserved it, but it was still the last thing she wanted to hear.

And in front of Harlan, no less.

"I'm sorry, Father."

They had settled down in the parlor, a pot of fresh coffee between them. Grace and Prissy had disappeared into the kitchen to clean up the breakfast dishes, but Maddie had a feeling they were standing on the other side of the door with their ears pressed against it.

"I don't think I'm the only one you owe an apology."

She turned to face Harlan, her chin tucked against her chest. "I'm truly sorry, Harlan. I didn't mean any harm."

"You know I forgive you." He smiled and warmed her heart.

"Now." Her father rubbed his hands together in eagerness. "Let's get down to wedding talk."

Maddie's chin jerked up, her gaze landing on her father. "What? Wedding talk?"

"Isn't that what this has all been about?" Pa asked.

"You're not angry with me?"

"I think you've learned your lesson. You should know better than to divulge in the fanciful. You went there to get a love potion, and instead you got ground vanilla bean and nutmeg. I say that's a small price to pay to relearn what you already knew."

"Ground vanilla—"

Her father gave her an indulgent smile. "You didn't really think Miss Farley gave you a real love concoction?"

She let out a choked laugh. "Of course not." The lie was so blatant, she was surprised her father didn't make her ask for forgiveness right there on the spot.

Instead, he continued. "She has to make money when she can."

"So you're not even upset with her?"

"One can't blame the snake oil salesman, for without the buyer, how will the salesman stay in business?"

She was chagrined. She looked to Harlan, who smiled as if to say, "I told you so."

"And you still want to marry me?" she asked.

Harlan's smile widened. "More than anything."

"Now," her father started again. "It seems that we

need a contract of sorts. A verbal agreement will do just fine. When shall the wedding take place?"

"In the spring," Harlan said before she could so much as take a breath to respond. "Is that all right with you?"

She smiled. "The spring will be lovely."

"I assume that you will be able to provide for my daughter, keeping her in a decent house and providing for her every need."

Harlan nodded. "That's why it has taken me so long to come and ask for her hand. I wanted to make sure my practice would flourish and I could provide. I'm looking to buy a parcel of land on the other side of the county, not too far out of town. Once the weather turns toward the warm, we can start building a house."

Maddie gasped, the reality of his feelings coming home. He did love her. Even after all her silly mistakes and crazy notions of making him fall in love with her, he still loved her.

"Are you all right, my dear?" Harlan turned toward her, concern on his brow.

"I'm just so happy," she said.

He smiled and took her hand. The warmth of his palm seeped into her skin. Love for her lit his blue eyes like the stars twinkling in the clear nighttime sky. How could one person be this happy? How could she have ever doubted that he loved her?

"Spring it is." Her father slapped his hands against his legs, his own joy evident. "God is good," he said, smiling at the two of them.

"Did we hear there's going to be a wedding this spring?" Grace and Prissy rushed into the room, raising the excitement level twofold.

"In the spring." Maddie nodded, her smile so wide her cheeks hurt. She never could have asked for more than this, would never even have dreamed she could be this happy.

Her sister and Prissy clasped hands with her, and together the three of them embraced and danced in a little circle of joy.

"Well, there is one thing I must do first." Harlan's words fell like a clump of wet clay in the middle of the room.

The girls stilled their feet and waited for him to continue. Somehow the excitement dimmed.

The room grew quiet and expectant as he stood and smoothed down the lapels of his suit. The action seemed to take forever as Maddie waited for him to reveal the one thing that would have to come before their wedding.

His eyes still sparkled but had turned darker than she had ever seen them. He walked to her and took her hands from the others' grasps and led her closer to the Christmas tree that had been set next to the window.

"Maddie," he said, his voice a little like an old bullfrog. He cleared his throat, dropped to one knee, and started again. "Maddie." He reached into his suit coat pocket and extracted the small box as he had the night before. "I have loved you since the first time I saw you standing by your father and welcoming the congregation to church. Ever since then, I have worked and toiled with one goal in mind: asking you to be my wife."

Maddie's heart pounded as she listened to his words. His confession was real this time. Well, it had been real the other two times before, but this time she knew it was real. Her hand trembled as he squeezed her suddenly cold fingers.

"Now the time has come. Maddie Sinclair, with your father's blessing, will you do me the honor of being my wife?"

"Yes," she whispered as happy tears spilled down her cheeks.

"I would like to present you with this," Harlan continued, releasing her fingers to take the lid from the ornate box. The beautiful cameo lay there, still nestled in the burgundy velvet. "It belonged to my grand-mother. I want you to wear it with the knowledge that you are loved."

"I will." She tugged him to his feet. "Always," she murmured as he wrapped his arms around her. "Always and forever."

Her family surrounded them, oohing and aahing at the cameo and the love found on this Christmas Day.

"Look," Prissy said, pointing out the window. "It's snowing again."

Grace smiled at the happy couple. "Looks like we'll have the rest of the day to make wedding plans."

Maddie's heart melted a little more as Harlan smiled. "Make sure that plan includes one of those fancy new wedding cakes I've been hearing about," he said.

"Oh," Maddie gushed, certain she would be the first bride in all of Calico Falls with such a fancy offering.

"I'll get a paper and pencil and we can work out all the details," Prissy said, starting for the desk.

"Just one thing," Harlan said, stopping her in her tracks. "The wedding cake can be as big as you want, but no gingerbread."

Common Gingerbread Cookie

Recipe from Miss Leslie's *Seventy-Five Receipts* (1827)

1 pint of molasses
1 pound of fresh butter
3 pounds of flour, sifted

a small teaspoonful of pearl
ash [cream of tartar] or less
a teacup of ginger, or more
if it is not strong

Cut the butter into the flour. Add the ginger. Having dissolved the pearl ash [cream of tartar] in a little vinegar, stir it with the molasses alternately into the other ingredients. Stir it very hard for a long time, till it is quite light. Knead it a little.

Put some flour on your paste-board, take out small portions of the dough, and make it with your hand into long rolls. Then curl up the rolls into round cakes, or twist two rolls together, or lay them in straight lengths or sticks side by side, and touching each other. Put them carefully into buttered pans, and bake them in a moderate oven, not hot enough to burn them. If they should get scorched, scrape off with a knife, or grater, all the burnt parts, before you put the cakes away.

You can, if you choose, cut out the dough with tins, in the shape of hearts, circles, ovals, etc., or you may bake it all in one and cut it in squares when cold.

If the mixture appears to be too thin, add, gradually, a little more sifted flour.

About the Author

Amy Lillard is a 2013 Carol Award–winning author for romance. She received this honor for her novel *Saving Gideon*, set in the Amish country of Oklahoma. *Saving Gideon* is book 1 of the Clover Ridge Series. Her other Clover Ridge titles include *Katie's Choice* and *Gabriel's Bride*. Her new trilogy, the Wells Landing Series, begins with *Caroline's Secret*, releasing in August 2014. Amy is a member of American Christian Fiction Writers and Romance Writers of America. Born and bred in Mississippi, she now lives in Oklahoma with her husband of twenty-five years and their teenage son. Amy can be reached at amylillard@hotmail.com and www.amywritesromance.com.

The Fruitcake Bride

by Vickie McDonough

Chapter 1

Bakerstown, Missouri
December 1890

Sitting on the edge of her seat, Karen Briggs wiped the dust off the train window with her handkerchief and searched the crowded depot for her fiancé. With a loud hiss, the train shuddered to a stop. She'd had the whole journey to ponder her decision to marry Clay Parsons. Had she made the right choice?

No matter. It was too late to turn back now. She donned her cloak, snatched up her satchel, and hurried to the door.

The conductor grinned as he bent and picked up the stepstool that rested beside the door. "You must be meetin' a feller to be so eager."

"My fiancé. He's the pastor of Bakerstown Chapel."

"Is he that Parson Parsons I've heard about?"

Karen blinked at the odd moniker. "Um. . .well, he *is* Pastor Clayton Parsons." Behind her, several other passengers lined up to exit. With so few debarking, why was such a large crowd gathered at the depot? Perhaps someone had a big family.

The conductor opened the door, allowing in a gush of chilly air. He stepped out and set the stool in place, but when he reached up to help her down, Clay rushed forward. "Please, sir, allow me."

Karen's apprehension fled, and her heart leaped like a young filly in a field of daisies as her intended smiled up at her. "Clay!"

He lifted her to the platform and into his arms for a brief hug then set her down and moved her out of the way of the other passengers. His blue-green eyes roamed her face as if looking for change. "I'm so glad you came."

She hoped she would be happy here—could make him happy. "It seems like years since you last left Arcadia instead of months."

Clay stepped back but held on to one of her elbows. A group of people crowded around them, most wearing bright smiles and all staring at her. Karen touched her hair to see if the pins had come loose. Two women toward the back of the crowd lifted up a sign that said: WELCOME!

"These kind people are some of my parishioners.

They were eager to meet you and welcome you to Bakerstown."

Karen smiled, even though disappointment coursed through her. She'd hoped for some time with Clay alone to discuss their arrangement, but being the future wife of a pastor, she knew she had to be gracious and share him. Her gaze traveled the crowd. She hoped most of these people would soon become her friends. "Thank y'all so much. It's very kind of you to come."

Clay made quick introductions then left her with the church people while he made arrangements for her two trunks to be delivered to the boardinghouse, where he'd secured a room for her.

"We just love Pastor Clay. He's such a fine young man—and handsome, too."

Was she Miss Herbert or Mrs. Wells? Karen grappled for the right name, but it flew away like a spooked bird.

"Hush, Emma Lou. She'll think you've got designs on her fiancé." A buxom woman holding one end of the sign fanned her face in spite of the chilly day.

"Why I never." Emma Lou's cheeks grew red as beet juice. "He's young enough to be my son."

"If you *had* a son," a man in back hollered in a good-natured tone.

A gentleman in a suit squeezed through the crowd, followed by a woman holding one of the sign poles.

"Emmett, slow down." She tugged on the pole as she moved forward, and a loud rip echoed across the platform as the banner split in two. Both women holding the poles stumbled.

Karen swallowed the lump in her throat, hoping the ruined sign wasn't a premonition of things to come.

"Mother, really." A pretty woman, who looked to be Karen's age, caught the toppling woman. "Must you always make a scene?"

"I declare, Helen. You've ruined the sign." The woman in back holding the other pole pursed her lips and shook her head.

"I didn't do it on purpose, Loraine." Helen straightened her bonnet.

"Never mind, ladies. We don't need a sign to welcome Miss Briggs to Bakerstown." Emmett stepped forward, hat in hand, along with Helen, still holding the stick and torn sign. "I'm Emmett Willard, mayor of Advent and a church council member, and this is my lovely wife, Helen."

He motioned to the younger woman who'd caught Helen. She stepped forward, eyeing Karen as if she were a maggot. Someone—or something—sure had put a wasp under her petticoat.

Mr. Willard cleared his voice, drawing Karen's gaze back to him. "This is our lovely daughter, Prudence."

"Prudy, Papa."

He sent her a patronizing smile with a warning in his gaze. "Prudy then. Miss Briggs, we're happy that you've finally arrived and hope you'll enjoy living in our small town."

Prudy snorted, yanking Karen's gaze back to her. The woman covered up her action with a quick cough.

Shifting her feet, Karen wasn't sure what to make of the pretty blond woman. She reminded herself to stay in a gracious mood and turned away from Prudy. "Thank you, Mr. Willard. It's so nice of everyone to take time from your busy schedules to greet me. I look forward to getting to know each of you."

Heads nodded, smiles abounded, and Karen relaxed a smidgeon. She must have said the right thing. Learning to be a pastor's wife might be harder than she had expected. She didn't want to do or say anything that could harm Clay's ministry in Bakerstown.

Clay rushed to her side, eyes twinkling like the ocean in sunlight. "I've taken care of your luggage. Would you like to go to the boardinghouse now?"

Tired from the long day's journey and stress of her

situation, Karen nodded. Even though she truly appreciated meeting some of the church people, she hoped the crowd wouldn't accompany them.

Clay looked over the group, smiling wide. "I can't thank you enough for coming out to greet Karen. It was mighty kind of y'all. I know she'd like to talk with each of you, but as you can see, she's exhausted from her travels."

"It's all right, Pastor." An older man on the left, leaning heavily on a cane, stepped forward. "We know you two young'uns need time alone." He winked at Karen, and her cheeks warmed.

Prudy crossed her arms and glared at her.

"We have a dinner reception planned for Sunday after church," Mrs. Willard said. "You'll get to meet the rest of our church family and try some of our Prudy's rhubarb pie."

Karen certainly hoped Prudy's pie was sweeter than her disposition.

"Thanks again for coming out today." Clay shook Mr. Willard's hand and several other men's.

The crowd began to disperse, and the man who'd winked at her hobbled up to them and leaned on his cane. "It was a pleasure to meet you, Missy. Parson Parsons sure landed himself a purty bride."

Clay beamed. "You're right about that, Jasper. Thank you for meeting the train."

"Happy to do so." He smiled a gap-toothed grin then turned and shuffled toward the stairs.

"Parson Parsons?" Karen turned to Clay and teasingly lifted one eyebrow.

A warm grin lifted his lips as he shrugged. "It's sort of an endearment some of the men use."

"It was kind of them to greet me, but is it awful of me to say I'm glad they left?"

"Of course not." He offered his elbow. "They were eager to meet you, but they respect our need to be alone."

She glanced at the train and saw two children with their noses to the window. "We aren't alone."

Clay waved at the two boys and smiled. "C'mon, let's get you settled at the boardinghouse and then eat some supper. I know you've got to be tired after your long trip across Missouri."

As he led her toward the depot steps, Karen surveyed what she could see of the small town. It looked to have only about a dozen streets with businesses lining the closest ones and then houses on the outer streets. "Where's your church?"

Clay paused at the top of the steps and pointed to the

southeast. "If you look two streets over and across the tops of the buildings, you can see the steeple." He turned to face her, looking uncertain. "The church isn't very big—only about twenty-five families."

Karen patted his arm. "Size doesn't matter. Arcadia wasn't very big either, but it was a fine town. I'm sure Bakerstown is too."

"You don't think you'll regret moving here?"

She hoped not, but then she had no other option. "My home is with you now."

He gave her a quick hug. "I'm glad you feel that way. I have to admit being a bit worried you'd change your mind."

The tension drained from her in light of his warm welcome. Maybe things *would* work out. "I might miss climbing Pilot Knob in the summer and feeling the cool air wafting up from the mine shafts."

"There were times this past summer I wished I was back home to enjoy that with you. It was quite hot here."

She tugged her cloak closed as a gust of cool air blew across the depot. "We don't have to worry about the heat now. Not with Christmas in just a few weeks."

"Will you be able to be ready for a Christmas Eve wedding?" Clay asked as he helped her down the stairs to the street.

"I should be." If she could lose her anxiety about marrying Clay because of her situation.

"And you're not sorry we're not marrying in Arcadia?"

"I would have enjoyed having our friends there, but your parents are coming, aren't they?"

He nodded. "Ma's last letter stated they would arrive on the twenty-third. I just wish your aunt was still around to see you married. She would have been proud."

Aunt Alice would have been delighted to hear she was marrying Clay Parsons, but not so happy with their marriage of convenience—or rather marriage of desperation. With her aunt deceased and the house for sale, she had no other options—and Clay needed a wife. She hoped their long friendship was a strong enough foundation for marriage.

"I'm glad you finally agreed to my proposal. I was starting to lose hope."

"I know a good thing when I see it." She couldn't resist teasing him, as she had so often in the past. His friendship had been one of the best things about moving to Arcadia to live with her aunt.

Clay tugged her closer as they crossed the street. "You're a wise woman."

"Wise enough to nab the preacher." She smiled up at him.

Maybe things would work out, after all.

Chapter 2

Karen closed the door to her room and leaned against it, smiling. The past hour and a half spent catching up with Clay had been wonderful. Their friendship seemed as close as ever. He'd been the big brother she never had, and that was one thing that concerned her about marrying him. She knew she loved Clay, but was it a romantic love? A love strong enough to endure a lifetime of marriage?

She'd also feared their long separation might have caused him to care less for her, but that wasn't the case, if the warm gaze in his eyes was an indication of his feelings.

Only a few more weeks, and she'd be his wife. She needed to find a way to rid herself of her doubts. Clay seemed excited about their marriage, and she knew she'd never find a better man.

She crossed the room to the desk where her satchel sat, but her eyes landed on something hidden behind it. A package wrapped in brown store paper and tied with twine. She tugged the note free and read it out loud. "A present for your kitchen, to be used when mixin'. With affection, Clay."

Curious, she untied the twine and unwrapped the gift. She lifted up the smallest of the three tan mixing bowls that had a blue accent line around it. Clay must be craving some of the sweets she used to bake for him back in Arcadia. She placed the bowl with its mates, thankful for the gift but wishing it had been a bit more romantic. But the man she was marrying was highly practical, and that was one thing about him she admired. And more than likely, one of the reasons he'd proposed.

Karen wandered over to the window that looked out onto Main Street. She hoped to catch a glimpse of Clay as he walked back to the parsonage, but the street was empty. As she leaned against the cool glass, her insecurities came storming back. She knew her lack of trust stemmed from her father's abandonment, leaving her at her aunt's shortly after her mother died. She'd been a scared, confused girl of eight, but then Clay had entered her life and become her best friend—her protector. He would never desert her like her father had.

Karen yawned and turned away from the window, ready to crawl in bed. As she removed her dress, her concerns taunted her. What if she wasn't gracious enough or lost her temper with the women of the church over some petty issue? And could she make Clay happy? Did she really have it in her to be the wife he needed?

⤬

Clay pried loose one of the trim boards around the window the Langston twins had broken on Sunday after church and tossed it to the ground. Carefully, he removed the broken glass and dropped it into a bucket, where it shattered into smaller pieces. He cleaned the area around the pane, installed the new piece of glass, and then reaffixed the trim. The new addition gleamed in the morning sunlight, filling Clay with a sense of accomplishment.

"It's a blessing that you're so handy with tools."

He glanced over his shoulder, glad to see Karen. "Why is that?"

"It must save the church a lot of money."

Clay climbed down, pondering her statement. Was Karen concerned that he couldn't adequately provide for her? She had lived with her widowed aunt, who'd been left somewhat well off after her husband's passing. "If I hadn't repaired it, someone else in the church would have stepped up and done it."

"Oh." Karen's smile dimmed. "I hadn't thought of that. My aunt always hired out any work she needed done, so I assumed you'd have to also."

"I prefer to see to most of the repairs to the church and parsonage—at least I do if I have the time."

"Well, you did an excellent job."

"Thank you." Clay warmed under his fiancée's approval. Ever since Karen moved to Arcadia to live with her aunt, he'd been her champion. She'd been so sad at first, missing her ma and constantly looking for her pa to return—but he never had. Clay eyed the basket she held over her arm. "What do you have in there?"

"I thought since it was such a nice day today, maybe we could have a picnic. Mrs. Grady was kind enough to fix an extra sandwich for you."

Clay smiled. "Having lunch with you sounds like a delight."

Karen ducked her head, her cheeks turning a comely shade of red. "It won't be long before we'll enjoy every meal together."

Clay glanced around and realized they were alone. He stepped closer and ran his index finger along Karen's soft cheek. "I can't tell you how much I look forward to that."

"Really?" She stared up at him, looking less sure

than he wished. Was she having doubts?

He'd prayed about their marriage so much and felt certain it was God's will for them. "Of course. I've been dreaming of the day."

Determined to prove his affection, he made sure they were alone then swooped in for a quick kiss.

"Clay!" Karen hastily looked around. "What would people say if they saw the pastor spooning?"

He chuckled. "I doubt they'd say anything unless I was spooning with someone other than you."

She playfully smacked his arm. "You'd better not be."

He gently pulled her close again. "Karen, how can I prove to you that there's no one on God's earth that I care to marry other than you?"

She nibbled her lip and ducked her head. "I've wondered if one day you'll regret marrying me."

"I wish you could peek into my heart and see your name written there. I know you still struggle because your pa left you, but I will never leave you like that. I care too much for you."

"I believe you. I suppose I'm just nervous."

"Even if your aunt hadn't died suddenly, I would have asked you to marry me. It just wouldn't have been for a few more months."

"Truly?"

"Have I ever lied to you?"

She shook her head.

"Give your concerns to God, and everything will work out." He squeezed her hand and stepped back. Karen had always suffered with self-doubt, but she was a kindhearted person—the woman he'd grown to love. He would just have to prove to her that he meant what he said. "Let me put away my tools and wash up. Then we can eat."

Karen nodded and looked around. "What about under that tree? It's warmer today, but do you think it's too cool to sit outside?"

"Let's give it a try since there's no wind. If you get too chilly, we can go in the church."

After returning the tools and ladder to the shed behind the building, Clay found Karen on the side of the church that faced town and watched her arranging the food on a bench. He'd wanted to marry since before he went to college, and now that their wedding was close, the days until Christmas Eve seemed to be dragging by at half the speed of a normal day. If only she seemed less worried and more excited.

He plopped down on the bench next to her, and she handed him a plate with a ham sandwich, thick slice of cheese, a pickle, and three-fourths of an apple. Clay smiled. "It looks wonderful. Shall we pray?"

She nodded and bowed her head while he thanked God for the food and for bringing Karen to Bakerstown. He took a bite of the pickle first, since it was making his mouth water. "Mmm. . .delicious. So, what do you think of Bakerstown?"

"It's smaller than Arcadia, but it seems nice. Things were quiet last night, so I had no trouble getting to sleep."

"I imagine you were exhausted after the long trip here, meeting some of the church folk, and spending time with me."

"I was tired, but not from being with you."

He winked at her and took a bite of his sandwich.

"Do you have services on Sunday night?"

"No, just in the morning. Some of the ranchers and farmers have a ways to travel, so they head back afterward. On the first Sunday of each month, we have a potluck dinner after the service, and most folks stay for that."

"What a wonderful idea! That gives everyone time to socialize with friends whom they don't often see."

"That's true."

Karen stared out toward the open prairie. "Are you happy here? Do the people treat you nicely?"

Clay took hold of Karen's hand. "The people here are very kind. As in all towns, there are those who think they should be treated more special, but I can handle them."

"I'm glad to hear that. I was a bit concerned about the two women who carried the welcome sign after hearing how they chided one another."

"Helen Willard and Loraine Bodine are sisters who tend to snap at each other, especially when things go wrong."

"Sisters? Well, it helps to know that."

Clay finished his food, enjoying the view Karen made. Even with a hat on, her honey-blond hair glistened in the sunlight. He loved the way her brown eyes sparkled whenever she laughed or teased him, although she hadn't done much of that since her arrival. He'd been attracted to her since the day Karen first showed up in school, looking sad and frightened. Before long they became friends. He'd never considered marrying any other woman, and he hadn't regretted that decision.

"Why are you looking at me like that?"

Clay flashed a mischievous grin. "I'm not sure you want me to answer that question."

An embarrassed smile danced on her lips; then

she ducked her head.

He shouldn't tease her like that, but he couldn't resist. "How would you like to see the parsonage?"

Her head jerked up. "Do you think it's proper for us to be there together since we're not yet married?"

"I don't see why it's a problem. We'll just leave the door open and make a quick pass through so you can see the house and be thinking about what you might want to change."

"I'd love to as long as you're sure it's all right. I don't want to do anything to get you in trouble."

"You won't." He handed her the plate. "Thanks for bringing me lunch. It was a wonderful surprise."

"I couldn't stand the thought of not seeing you until this evening."

He smiled and helped her to her feet. "I can't tell you how happy that makes me."

After Karen packed the basket, Clay took it and escorted her the one block to the parsonage. He watched her face as her gaze landed on the small clapboard house painted a pale yellow with white trim.

"Oh Clay, it's lovely. I don't know what I expected, but it wasn't anything this nice."

He pulled back the screen door and propped it open with the basket then pushed on the main door.

"This is the parlor, and as you can see, the kitchen is on the left side. There are two bedrooms at the rear of the house and a small washroom."

Karen turned in a circle, taking everything in. Then she spun around to face him, eyes gleaming. "Oh Clay, I love it."

Basking in her pleasure, he wasn't prepared when she threw herself into his arms. He quickly wrapped his arms around her, but he stumbled backward until he bumped into the wall. Karen kissed him soundly, and his arms tightened as he enjoyed her closeness.

A loud gasp from the porch made him realize they were no longer alone. Karen jumped away, and he straightened to look into the shocked eyes of Helen Willard and her daughter.

"Pastor, what is the meaning of this?"

Chapter 3

Karen wished she were a bird that could fly away and hide in the trees. She and Clay weren't even married yet, and she was already causing trouble for him. What had gotten into her to kiss him like she had?

He shifted his feet. "Nothing quite as terrible as you're imagining happened, Mrs. Willard."

The woman narrowed her eyes. "I know what I saw."

Prudence stood behind her mother, arms crossed, looking as if she were ready to do battle, but Karen wasn't sure whose side the young woman was on. Was she upset with her mother? Or with Clay and her?

He cleared his throat. "What you saw was Karen expressing her delight at seeing the lovely parsonage we'll be sharing. I just showed her the parlor and kitchen so she could make plans for when this is her home."

Mrs. Willard crossed her arms. "Humph! Looked more like a young couple seeking a private place to spark."

Prudy's face grew red, but she remained quiet.

"One kiss does not a spark make." Clay smiled as if trying to lessen the tension.

The woman narrowed her eyes again. "No matter. It is inappropriate behavior for a pastor and a poor example for my impressionable daughter. You can be certain the church council will hear of this."

"Perhaps it would be best for Miss Briggs to return to her hometown and come back here just before the wedding." Prudence lifted her chin.

Karen's mouth opened, but nothing came out at the woman's unexpected suggestion. She thought of all she had to do in the few weeks before the wedding and knew it wouldn't get done if she were in Arcadia worrying about Clay. And she really had no home to return to since she'd sold her aunt's furniture and belongings and had listed the house for sale with an agent.

"I don't think we need to go to such extremes, Miss Willard."

Prudence batted her long lashes at Clay. "I told you to call me Prudy."

Her mother elbowed her. "That is inappropriate, Prudence."

The young woman scowled at her mother but turned a pout Clay's way. "I'm sure Clay is able to make up his own mind about that, Mother."

"Never mind." Mrs. Willard swatted her hand at her daughter. "The point is they shouldn't have been spooning in the parsonage."

"I can assure you, ma'am, it won't happen again." Clay shuffled his feet.

"You two should have considered that before making such a spectacle."

Karen couldn't let Clay take the blame for something she initiated. Wringing her hands, she took a step toward the woman. "Mrs. Willard, Clay is right. My joy at finding such a lovely place to call home overwhelmed me, and I expressed my delight by kissing him. Once. I'm the one who bears the blame, not him."

Mrs. Willard didn't seem to be wavering, so she tried another tactic. "Surely you were young and in love not so long ago."

Clay snorted but then rubbed his nose, looking chagrined. Prudence rolled her eyes as Karen struggled to maintain an innocent gaze.

Mrs. Willard looked from Karen to Clay and back then sighed. "I suppose I was. But you two shouldn't be alone like this. It'll set loose lips to talkin'."

Clay nodded. Karen stepped out onto the porch, and he followed, closing the door.

"Well, now that Miss Briggs has seen the house,

there's no reason for her to be in there again until after you've said your vows."

"Yes ma'am," they said in unison.

Mrs. Willard lifted her chin. "I will overlook it this time, but don't let it happen again."

"Thank you." Clay took hold of Karen's arm and started toward the steps but paused. "Was there something that brought you two here today?" he asked Mrs. Willard.

"Prudence made some lovely curtains for your kitchen, but we can return another time to put them up." She spun, nose in the air, and hurried down the sidewalk.

Prudence remained where she was, her gaze focused on Karen. "You might want to consider going back"—she waved her hand in the air—"to wherever it is you came from. Clay could benefit from marrying a woman from these parts, not someone who knows nothing about this town."

Karen gasped.

Scowling, Clay stepped in front of her. "Miss Willard, I told you more than once that I am not an eligible man. My heart belongs to Karen and always has. It's time you face that fact."

Hurt engulfed Prudy's pretty face, and she stomped

her foot. She spun around, skirts flying, and followed her mother back to the street.

Clay took hold of Karen's hand. "I'm so sorry about that. I thought that if I continued to inform Pru— Miss Willard—of my relationship with you, she'd finally take a hint, but she can be hardheaded." He escorted her off the porch. "I'd best see you back to the boardinghouse, and then I need to visit several ill parishioners."

Karen watched Prudence disappear around the far side of the church; then she turned to Clay. "I'm so sorry for getting you in trouble."

"Don't worry about it. Mrs. Willard is quick to make a mountain out of a molehill." He frowned. "Maybe I shouldn't say that, but it's the truth, and you need to be aware of it."

"Do you really think she'll keep quiet about seeing us kissing in the parsonage?"

He shrugged. "Time will tell."

"I'm sorry for my rash behavior."

Grinning, Clay looped her arm around his. "I'm not in the least."

Secretly happy with his declaration, Karen prayed the women would not gossip about what they saw. Prudence was certainly an odd duck. Did she really think she could sway Karen into leaving?

Karen determined to put the disastrous duo from her mind and enjoy her remaining minutes with Clay. "Would you like me to go with you on your visitations?"

"After we're married, I think it would be a wonderful idea, unless someone is sick with something that spreads. I'd hate for you to become ill."

She bit back a smile, but it broke loose. "Because you don't want to have to nurse me back to health?"

With a playful gleam in his gaze, Clay waggled his eyebrows. "That would be my pleasure, ma'am, but I would prefer you not get ill in the first place."

Not ready to consider such an intimate situation, Karen studied the spacious yard, a thought percolating. "Do you suppose we could get some chickens?"

Clay grinned. "That was a quick change of topic. Why chickens?"

Karen watched a trio of sparrows swoop down and snatch something on the ground and then fly up into the tree again. "I thought it might be nice if I made chicken soup for the church members who are sick or injured."

"You'd go through your flock of hens pretty fast."

"Well, perhaps I could make potato soup or stew sometimes."

"We'll see. It's a very kind gesture, but I don't want you cooking for others all the time."

"Oh? Who *would* you like me cooking for?"

"Who do you think?" He squeezed her hand then pulled a small, oblong package from his pocket. "That reminds me, here's a little something I got for you."

"I love the bowls you left in my room, by the way." She smiled. "You don't need to give me another gift."

"I want to give you nice things. I enjoy it."

Karen sighed. "I appreciate it, but I want you to know it's not necessary."

He held out the package. "Humor me."

She unwrapped the small gift and stared at the odd metal object. "What is it?"

"Haven't you ever seen a nutcracker? Now you won't have to stomp on shells or hit them with a hammer."

"I remember how much you enjoy nuts, especially in my fruitcake. Thank you. This will come in handy." Another odd gift, but the gleam in her fiancé's eyes made her smile. She saw Mrs. Grady sweeping off the porch and realized they were back at the boardinghouse.

"I'm glad you like it." He bent down and placed a quick kiss on the back of her hand. "I'll see you at supper."

With a sigh, Karen watched him stride away, tall and lithe.

Mrs. Grady leaned against the porch railing. "That pastor is a fine-looking man. I imagine the two of you will have comely young'uns."

Karen spun around, stunned by her landlady's comment. "I. . .uh. . .thank you."

Mrs. Grady chuckled. "Don't look so shocked. It's merely the truth. Just watch out for that Prudence Willard. She set her cap for the parson the day he arrived." Mrs. Grady clucked her tongue and shook her head. "Poor thing didn't know the pastor's heart was already spoken for."

Heat rising to her cheeks, Karen climbed the steps to the porch. No wonder Prudy had eyed her so maliciously. The woman had hoped to marry Clay. How could Karen blame her? Clay was a wonderful man, and any woman would be happy to have him for a husband. He was quickly winning her over and making her realize that in spite of the circumstances surrounding their upcoming marriage, he was the man for her.

Her thoughts veered back to Mrs. Grady's comment about her and Clay's children. She *had* on occasion contemplated marrying him when she was younger and wondered what their children might look like, but to hear it expressed out loud was a surprise. Karen glanced to her side to discover the landlady had resumed her sweeping. "Do you need any help with dinner? I seem to have the afternoon free."

"Heavens, no! I don't allow guests to assist with the meals."

"Please, I'd like to help."

Mrs. Grady continued shaking her head. "I'm sure you must have some preparations for your wedding that need to be done."

Karen sighed. "I do have some sewing, although it's not my favorite task."

"Best you get it over and done with then." She placed the broom in the corner of the porch and scurried toward the door, pausing just inside. "Make sure you know that pastor of yours is welcome to supper. No sense in you two eating at the café when your meals are included with your room and board."

"But Clay's aren't."

"It's a sad day when there isn't enough to feed my pastor." She turned and disappeared inside the house.

Karen leaned against the porch railing, wishing Clay had let her go with him. The long afternoon stretched out in front of her, and the thought of spending it sewing alone failed to excite her. But she had a new nightgown to finish stitching—the gown she'd wear on her wedding night. Thoughts of that evening brought warmth to her cheeks.

∞

Karen swallowed back her anxiety as she approached the Willard home. Clay had encouraged her to attend the sewing bee, and although several of the church ladies had invited her, neither Mrs. Willard nor her daughter had mentioned it or sent an invitation. Three days had passed since she'd visited the parsonage with Clay. Would Mrs. Willard use this opportunity to announce to the ladies that she'd seen Karen and the pastor kissing?

A woman who looked to be around Karen's age waved. She rushed across the dirt street and made a beeline toward her, smiling and carrying a small basket. "Good morning. You must be the pastor's intended." She stopped in front of Karen. "I'm Patricia Mullins, but most folks call me Patsy."

"I'm Karen Briggs. It's a pleasure to meet you."

Patsy's hazel eyes sparkled. "I always enjoy these gatherings. It's such fun to sit and talk with other women. My husband, Jared, is a quiet man and doesn't have much to say, and we don't have children yet." Her fair complexion turned ruby red, making her freckles stand out. "I'm glad you came. It'll help even the odds between the older and younger women."

Karen smiled and eyed the front of the big brick

294

house, one of the largest in town.

"Don't let the size of the place intimidate you. The ladies are always welcoming, but be warned, they'll most likely bombard you with questions." Patsy paused at the steps and smiled. "Shall we go in?"

She nodded and followed her new friend up to the porch, glad she didn't have to enter alone. Patsy knocked, and Mrs. Willard opened the door quickly, as if she'd been hovering there, waiting for them.

"Miss Briggs, it's nice of you to join us today, and it's always good to see you, Patsy." She stepped back, allowing them to enter.

As Karen's eyes adjusted to the interior lighting, she marveled at the lovely furnishings. "You have a beautiful home, Mrs. Willard."

"Thank you. Emmett does like to spoil me." She waved her hand to a room on the right. "We're gathering in the study."

Patsy took hold of Karen's arm and tugged her into the room. Three women were seated on the far side of a colorful wedding ring quilt, while two others had claimed spots on the right. Patsy led Karen around to the left side, where three chairs awaited. They took the farthest two, leaving the one beside Karen empty.

"I imagine some of you have met Pastor Parsons's

bride-to-be, but in case you haven't, this is Karen Briggs," Patsy stated, as if they were lifelong friends.

Most of the women smiled and eyed Karen with curiosity. She recognized Loraine, who'd help hold the welcome sign, although she'd forgotten her last name. Karen nodded. "It's a pleasure to meet you."

"This here's Lois Clemmons." Patsy pointed to the nearest lady and continued down the line and around the corner. "Gertrude Birch, Loraine Bodine, Sue Ellen Smith, and Paulette Davis."

Karen tried to put names and faces together. Gertrude and Loraine looked to be about the same age as Mrs. Willard, probably in their late forties or early fifties, while Sue Ellen and Paulette were at least a decade younger.

Paulette smiled. "Don't bother trying to learn our names today. We know it will take a while to remember us all."

"I appreciate that."

Patsy sat, so Karen did, too.

"This is a lovely quilt. Have you made many together?"

"This is our seventh one," Loraine said.

"Isn't it our eighth?" Mrs. Willard stood near the study door, tapping her upper lip with her index finger.

"Let's see, we've auctioned off three of them to raise money for the church and orphanage, gave one to the Henrys for their fortieth anniversary, one to the Garfields for their twenty-fifth, and one to Spencer and Julia Sloan when he retired as mayor two years ago."

"That's still just seven, Helen, counting this new one." Loraine lifted her chin.

A knock at the door sent Mrs. Willard spinning away. Karen had the feeling she was glad not to have to respond to Loraine.

A pretty young woman entered and claimed the seat next to Karen. She smiled. "I'm Carla Peterson."

"Karen Briggs. A pleasure to meet you."

"She's Pastor Parsons's intended," Gertrude stated.

Loraine rolled her eyes. "Everyone knows who she is. She's the only new woman in town."

Soft chuckles wafted around the room then suddenly quieted. All eyes turned toward the entrance. Prudence moseyed in, overdressed in her rust-colored afternoon dress with huge leg o' mutton sleeves and a bib of ruffles and lace that covered her bodice. She narrowed her eyes at Karen and took the farthest away empty seat. Confused by the woman's obvious dislike for her, Karen looked down at the quilt. Was it true that Prudence had designs on Clay? That would explain her unwarranted hostility, as well as her suggestion for Karen to return to Arcadia.

Helen sat next to her daughter. "Thelma won't be here today. Her three young'uns are ill."

"I hope it's nothing serious," Paulette said.

Helen shrugged. "I don't know what's wrong."

All around Karen, baskets clattered as the ladies removed their scissors, needles, and thread. She stared at the beautiful quilt, half afraid to apply her hand. What if her stitches were too large or not uniform?

Carla leaned over. "Don't be nervous about stitching. We all had a first day, too. Just jump right in."

"If Helen isn't happy, she'll redo the stitches anyway," Patsy whispered in her ear. Several ladies to Patsy's left nodded their agreement.

Wonderful. Now she had to worry about her sewing pleasing Mrs. Willard when they'd already gotten off to a rough start. Determined to do her best, Karen pulled out a small container and removed a quilting needle. Patsy handed her a piece of thread, and she pushed the end through the eye and found a spot to begin stitching.

"So, Miss Briggs. Where did you and Pastor meet?"

Karen glanced up, not quite sure which lady had asked the question, but by the gazes pointed at her, she suspected everyone was interested in her answer. "After my mother died, when I was eight, I went to live in Arcadia with my widowed aunt. Clay was in the school I started attending."

A smile softened Loraine's expression. "Was it love at first sight?"

Prudy looked as if she was sucking on an unsweetened lemon drop.

"No, not at all." Karen shook her head. "I felt so out of place and was missing my parents so badly that I hardly looked up from my desk for weeks. At first, Clay was one of the boys who pestered me, but I think he was just trying to pull me out of my shell."

Gasps filled the room.

"Our pastor was a hooligan?" Lois fanned her face.

"I find that hard to believe," Prudy said. "Pastor Clay is so kindhearted and courteous."

"He wasn't ever mean—just tugged on my braids and tried to get me to laugh. But at the time, I thought he was being a pest." She smiled, remembering the day she realized he wanted to be her friend. "Clay lived only a few houses from my aunt's home, so we eventually started walking to school together and became friends."

"And did he help you get over the loss of your mother?" Carla asked.

Karen thought for a moment. "I suspect he did indirectly. Becoming friends with Clay opened the door for me to be friends with the young people he knew, and that helped me to adjust to my new life in Arcadia." Still, she never forgot how her pa had deposited her at Aunt Alice's home shortly after her mother's death and never returned. She didn't even know if he was alive.

"So, you've known Pastor quite a long time. Why have you not married before now?" Loraine peeked up then glanced back down.

Karen eyed her own stitches, not liking how uneven they were. "Once Clay felt God calling him to the ministry, he left to go to college and then seminary. Afterward, he wanted to get established in his church." She hadn't realized what he meant to her until he was gone. For so long, she'd thought of him as a big brother, but as they grew older, at some point, her feelings for him shifted to something deeper. Yet until her aunt died suddenly, he had never asked her to marry him. She hadn't even known his thoughts drifted in that direction.

Patsy looked her way. "That's a long time to wait on a man. Were there no others who attempted to woo you?"

Karen shook her head. No man ever compared to Clay.

Prudy cleared her throat, drawing Karen's gaze. "But what about Clay? How do you know his feelings remained loyal after such a long separation?"

"Prudence! What an awful thing to say?" Helen turned ten shades of red.

In spite of her mother's reprimand, there was a challenge in Prudy's eyes that gave Karen pause. Had Clay merely asked her to marry him out of some sense of noble duty? There were the flashes of admiration in his gaze, and he'd even kissed her, so he must care for her. Clay wasn't the kind of man to fake his feelings. He was too honest—too good. Karen lifted her chin and aimed it at Prudy like a weapon, although she forced her tone to be civil. "Clay would never have asked me to marry him if he didn't care for me."

Prudy ducked her head, lips puckered, as if studying her stitches. Karen didn't want to hurt the young woman's feelings, but Prudy needed to know that her infatuation with Clay could lead nowhere.

Karen continued stitching and answering questions. Though the ladies were gracious, they were a curious lot. She was glad when they turned to the topic of Christmas and the annual auction supporting a Dallas orphanage.

Two hours later, Mrs. Willard pushed her chair

back, signaling an end to the sewing bee. "Shall we stop and enjoy the delicious cookies Sue Ellen brought?"

Heads nodded and murmurs filled the room as the women tied off their stitches and put their supplies away. Prudy made a quick escape. Karen studied her stitches. They resembled the path a staggering drunkard might take. Patsy and Carla had done an excellent job with their handwork. Karen had little doubt Helen would be redoing hers before next session. She watched the ladies on the end and far side of the table leave the room, happily chatting. Karen missed her Arcadia friends, but in time she'd make new ones here.

Sighing, she lifted her arm to reach for her basket, but not only her arm moved, the quilt rack did, too. Suspended from the ceiling by four ropes, it swung her direction. She instantly straightened, forcing the rack in the opposite direction. Patsy reached to steady it and missed. Karen watched horrified, as the rack knocked both Gurdy and Lois sideways. The two older women struggled to stay on their feet, but both toppled sideways onto vacant chairs. After taking a moment to regain their composure, the women gaped at Karen.

"I'm so sorry." She glanced at the quilt, her cheeks blazing hot. "It seems that I somehow basted the lace on my cuff to the quilt." She peered sideways at Patsy, who was struggling to keep a smile off her face. The other women were already filing out of the room, engrossed in their conversations, oblivious to what had happened.

"Well," Gurdy said, "the first time we attempted a quilt, Helen stitched her skirt to the bottom of it. We had to help her out of the garment in order to cut it loose."

Lois nodded in agreement, a glimmer in her pale blue eyes. The humor of the situation set Karen to giggling, and soon the other ladies were chuckling, too.

"As much as I hate to ask, I need help getting my sleeve free."

Patsy and Carla quieted, although both obviously struggled to hold back their laughter.

"I guess I know where Helen will be tonight," Karen mumbled.

Patsy snorted a laugh.

Gertrude helped Lois up. "We'll see you ladies in the parlor, and our lips are sealed."

As the two left the room, Patsy mumbled, "That'll be a first."

Carla giggled so hard she could barely hold her scissors still enough to clip the threads. "There. Try it now."

Karen lifted her arm, and this time her sleeve broke free. She tugged out the loose threads and stood.

"Thank you, Carla."

"Too bad the quilt rack is tied to the ceiling, otherwise we could turn it so Helen wouldn't notice." Patsy gave Karen a gentle nudge.

The three women giggled again as they made their way out of the room. In spite of her embarrassing mistake, Karen knew she'd made several new friends.

Chapter 4

On Sunday afternoon, Clay drove his buggy out of town. Karen sat next to him with a blanket covering their legs, glad to have him to herself on the cool but sunny day. "I enjoyed your sermon. You have such a lovely speaking voice."

He glanced at her, eyes twinkling. "You really think so—about the message, I mean."

"Of course I do. I wouldn't tease about something that important. You've matured since leaving Arcadia. Your sermons have more depth than when you were a youth, practicing in the field behind my aunt's home, but I'll always remember the passion you had then."

"Do you think I've lost some of that zeal?"

"No, that's not what I meant." Contemplating what to say next, Karen studied the wintry landscape as they traveled past farm after farm. Come spring, the rolling hills would blossom with wildflowers and be lovely. "You know how naive young men can be. They think they can conquer every dragon that dares to pop up its head."

"That's true. I certainly would have battled any be-hemoth that threatened you, my fair maiden."

He surprised Karen when he shifted the reins to his other hand and lifted his right arm, dropping it around her shoulders. "So, you're saying I've mellowed in my old age?"

"Yes, the ripe old age of twenty-three." Karen giggled and dared to lean against him, enjoying the closeness. But the memory of Prudy's snide comments and sneers threatened to ruin the lovely day. Karen had seen no special interest in Clay's eyes when he glanced at Prudy, but she obviously was smitten with him. Not that Karen could blame her.

He squeezed her shoulders. "Don't forget, ma'am, you're only a year behind me."

"We're positively ancient," she said, trying to regain her levity.

"Good thing we're getting married soon. If we waited much longer, I might have to carve you a cane for a wedding gift."

"You're funny." Karen smiled as she considered his most recent gift—a lovely quartet of teacups and sau-cers with a pretty violet design and a matching pot. "Speaking of gifts, I adored the tea set, but you know you don't have to keep giving me presents, don't you?"

He shrugged and tightened his grip as the buggy dipped into a rut and back out. "I enjoy it. I've never had much money—not that I have a lot now—but when I was younger and in seminary, I rarely had any. I want to make up for the times I was unable to get you a birthday gift."

Karen laid her head on Clay's shoulder. "How is it I'm so lucky to have won your affection?"

He caught her gaze and winked. "My heart has been yours since the day I first saw you."

Karen's heart somersaulted. Had he really cared for her for so long? She'd been hurting so badly back then that she hadn't noticed. "I don't know how you could have fallen for that scrawny, insecure girl I used to be." Although she had filled out to a respectable womanly form, the insecurities still plagued her. She loved Clay, too—and not in a brotherly way. Being with him again was helping her to see that, but it was her ability to be a pastor's wife that concerned her. Aunt Alice had taught her to cook and the basics of sewing, but her aunt had been a quiet woman who loved reading, so Karen had spent much of her time alone in her room. Large groups still made her anxious.

"Maybe I was attracted to you because you looked so scared and lonely. You needed a champion."

He had no idea how true that was. She was still scared, not so much of marrying him but of failing him. "You must have been desperate for friends."

"Don't say that." He paused for a long while then sighed and pulled the buggy to a halt. The horse snorted as if not ready to stop, but he obeyed. Clay shifted toward her, bumping his long legs against her skirts. "You're not having doubts about us, are you? Is my congregation pestering you too much? I know some of the ladies can be difficult."

"I won't lie to you. I had many doubts before coming here, but being with you and seeing how excited you are about our marriage has helped alleviate most of my concerns." Karen looked past him at several horses grazing in a field.

"But not all of them?"

She shook her head. "I worry that I don't have the skills to be a pastor's wife." *And about Prudence Willard.*

A red-tailed hawk swooped low, soaring over the horses before it landed on a fence post. Even with most of the foliage dried and yellow and the trees naked of their leaves, the countryside was still beautiful.

"Look at me, Karen."

She turned, giving him her full attention. His blue-green eyes focused on her, making her feel special—loved. "I have no doubt at all that you'll make a wonderful pastor's wife. You're kind and caring, patient—most of the time." He grinned when she elbowed his side. "You will have to overlook many things and try hard not to get angry when our church family intrudes on our private time, but I know you can."

Karen's heart warmed at his faith in her. Not since her mother died had anyone believed in her with the passion he did. "You're a good man, Parson Parsons."

He rolled his eyes. "Don't start with that. I might be tempted to steal a kiss just to silence you."

There had been times in the past when she'd wondered what his kiss would be like. Now that they'd shared a couple of quick, stolen kisses, she wanted to know what a real knee-bending one would be like—and she had it within her power to find out. Sheer delight wove its way through her like warm coffee on a cold morning. "Oh you would—Parson Par—"

He stopped her with his lips on hers, cold at first but quickly warming. Clay tugged her closer, illustrating his affection and pushing her doubts into the shadows of her mind. Oh how she loved this man—if only she could be enough.

Too soon, he pulled back. He caressed her cheek with his gloved hand. "I'd love nothing more than to keep kissing you, but it's not a wise idea, for now. Besides"—he smiled—"I've got a surprise. Now close your eyes."

Still rattled from his soul-stirring kisses, she blinked. "Another gift?"

"Not exactly. There's something special I want you to see, so be a good girl and comply. Eyes shut."

"Yes sir." When he faced forward again, Karen laid her head on his solid shoulder and lowered her eyelids. How could she be so fortunate to be betrothed to such a wonderful man?

They wound to the left on the country road and then back to the right. Karen listened to the rhythmic clatter of the wheels, the jingle of the harness, and tried to recognize the call of several birds she heard, all the while wondering what Clay wanted her to see. It couldn't be land for a home, because he would never want to live this far from town. As they wound around another curve, she heard flowing water.

The buggy creaked to a stop. "All right. You can look now."

Karen straightened, peered down the road, and gasped. Before her, a charming wooden bridge spanned a small river. Although there was a roof covering it, the sides rose only about four feet, allowing one to view the water. "A covered bridge?"

"It's called the Courting Bridge. Young fellows from these parts bring their gals out here to spoon or ask them to marry. I'm a little surprised we have the place all to ourselves."

She nudged him in the side, unable to resist teasing. "Which one are we here for?"

Clay chuckled. "Why, Miss Briggs, you do surprise me. Guess you'll have to wait and see."

He clucked out the side of his mouth, and the horse stepped into motion. Clay drove the buggy onto the bridge, the horse's hooves echoing on the wooden floor, and stopped. After setting the brake, he climbed out of the buggy and reached for her. She laid aside the blanket and let Clay help her down then took his arm as he led her to one side of the bridge.

Karen leaned against the wooden planks and looked down at the slowly moving water as it bumped over the vast collection of rocks. If the temperature had been warmer, she might have been tempted to climb down the bank and soak her feet. "Thank you for bringing me here, Clay. It's so peaceful."

He rested his hands on the wood railing. "Yes it is. I sometimes come here when I'm having trouble hearing from God about a sermon topic. I don't know if it's being out among God's creation or just getting away from the busyness of people and noise of the town, but I find I can hear Him at this place."

"I can understand, but why is there a covered bridge in the middle of nowhere? Who built it?"

"The official name is the Baxter Bridge, and it's over twenty years old. I heard an easterner built it because he wanted to propose to his beloved on a covered bridge like the one near her Vermont home."

"And did he?"

"As far as I know."

"What happened to them?"

"They must have married and moved away. I don't know anyone living in this county with the Baxter surname."

Karen shifted toward him. "The bridge is a nice legacy."

Clay nodded and took her hands. "So, are you sure you want to marry me and live in Bakerstown? It's just a small town, but the people are good, at least most of them are."

"Most of those I've met have been very kind, and the size of the town doesn't bother me."

Clay studied her face for a long moment. "Why do I hear hesitation in your voice?"

Karen shrugged and glanced at the river.

"Tell me. Whatever it is, we can work through it."

How could she express all her fears and reservations? Clay had always been focused—always known he wanted to be a pastor like his grandpa. Her life had been like a rudderless boat rocked and tossed on turbulent waters. Her aunt had taken Karen into her home after her pa had left her. She missed both parents so much. That grief had shaped her and made her less trusting and less sure of things. There'd been times she'd even doubted God's goodness and had ranted at Him when she was younger.

"Karen, what is it? Please tell me what's creating the confusion I see in your pretty face." Clay's brow wrinkled.

She hated the worry that flashed in his eyes.

"Have you changed your mind. . .about marrying me?"

She laid her gloved hand on his cheek, hoping to reassure him. "No, Clay. I care deeply for you, and I'm looking forward to being your wife. But like I told you, what if I do something wrong at one of the church events? It might cause you to lose your church after you've worked so hard. How could I live with myself if that happened?"

He blew out a sigh as the tension left his expression. "My career is in God's hands, not the church board's, so please stop worrying. Just be my wife and take care of me. I don't care if you don't have anything to do with the church other than attending the services, smiling at me, and giving a resounding *amen* every now and then."

She offered a tentative smile. "Maybe you wouldn't, but the church people would. They expect certain things of their pastor's wife." She ducked her head. "And everything I do seems to flop."

Clay pulled her into his arms. "I should have married you years ago. You always were a thinker, stewing on things, contemplating how something might work out or not. I believe that God called us to be together."

"I believe that, too, but I can't shake my doubts." Karen stepped back as a picture of pretty Prudy infiltrated her mind. "Everything I do is a failure. First, Mrs. Willard caught us kissing; then I sewed my sleeve to the quilt the Ladies Society is making. Why, even my welcome sign split in half."

Clay chuckled, and she smacked his chest. "Don't laugh. I'm serious."

"I'm sorry, sweetheart, but you have to admit that was rather humorous, watching Mrs. Bodine trying to keep up with Mrs. Willard."

"You're missing the point." She turned and walked back toward the buggy, upset at him for the first time since arriving in Bakerstown. His parents had cherished him. He was always secure in who he was and always knew what he wanted out of life. Clay had no idea what it was to struggle—to wonder if he was doing the right thing. She wouldn't be the cause of him losing his pastorate, even if it meant that she couldn't marry him. But the thought of possibly losing him made her heart crack.

"Karen, please. I'm sorry for laughing. You have to understand that those two ladies are always trying to outdo one another. Only one thing is important." He gently grabbed hold of her arms and turned her toward him, searching her features. "Do you love me?"

"You know I do. How could you doubt that?"

"You seem so troubled."

"It's my problem, not yours."

"That isn't true. You're a part of me already, sweetheart. When you hurt, I hurt." He took her hands again. "God will get us through the hard times. We just have to trust Him. *You* have to trust Him. Can you do that?"

She knew he spoke the truth. Even though she'd been mad at God for years for allowing her mother to die and her pa to leave, as she grew older, her faith in God and ability to lean on Him was what had gotten her through the difficult times she'd encountered and the long years of loneliness while Clay was gone to college and seminary. Prudy was merely another trial she must endure and survive. She smiled. "Yes, I believe I can do that."

He grinned, obviously happy with her response. "We're a good team—you, me, and the Lord. Remember the scripture, 'A threefold cord is not quickly broken'?"

She, Clay, and the Lord—a trifold braid. She latched onto the picture in her mind, and if she could only hang on to that image, maybe her life wouldn't unravel.

Chapter 5

Karen surveyed the nearly completed shirt she was making for Clay, which lay across her bed. She'd noticed his Sunday preaching shirt had dark stains on the collar and cuffs. He'd worn the same shirt both Sundays and several times during the week, so she assumed it was the only dress shirt he had and decided to attempt one for his Christmas present.

"It doesn't look half bad." Karen eyed one place that puckered where the left sleeve and shoulder met. "I can't thank you enough for your help, Patsy. I'd never have accomplished this without your guidance."

Patsy smiled as she put away her sewing supplies. "I'm glad to be of assistance. And besides, it gives me a reason to visit."

"You don't need a reason. Come anytime."

"Thank you. The same is true for you." Patsy bent over the shirt, examining it. "All you have left are the buttons and hem. Are you going to wait for Christmas or give it to him when it's done?"

Karen shrugged. "I originally thought Christmas—after we're married—but it would be nice for him to have a new shirt to wear now since there are several church events for the holidays."

"Not to mention your wedding." Patsy's eyes gleamed.

Karen touched her warm cheeks. Would she ever be able to talk about the wedding without blushing?

Patsy grinned. "I remember turning red like you do every time someone mentioned me and Jared gettin' hitched."

"How did you endure it? People sure seem to enjoy poking fun at courting couples, especially Clay and me."

Shrugging, Patsy smoothed a wrinkle in her skirt. "You have to understand that everyone in Bakerstown loves and respects Pastor Clay. The folks around here are happy for you and just wantin' to share in the fun. Folks in these parts work hard, so they need some fun and excitement and don't mind intrudin' on yours."

Some people may be happy for her and Clay, but Karen knew Prudy wasn't. Every time the woman laid eyes on Karen, she was scowling. "What can you tell me about Prudence Willard?"

Patsy stared at her with wide hazel eyes. "Why

would you ask about her?"

Karen lifted her eyebrows in a "Do I have to explain it?" expression.

Patsy sighed. "I guess you deserve to know the truth. I just hope it's not gossipin' to tell you." She gazed out the window for a moment then turned back. "Prudy is a lot like her mother. Helen is used to getting what she wants. Prudy is an only child, and she's had things lavished on her all her life. It's not exactly her fault she's the way she is, but that's beside the point."

Karen twisted her hands together. "But why does she look down on me? I've never done anything to her."

"You're marrying the man she planned to wed."

Karen gasped. "But how is that possible? Has Clay given her any special attention?"

Giving her a sympathetic look, Patsy shrugged. "I don't think so, but Pastor Clay came about the time Jared and I were married. We missed his first two Sundays here because we went home to Independence for the wedding. It's possible that Prudy took one look at him and decided to woo him."

"So, you've never seen Clay encourage her?"

"No. Not at all." Patsy reached over and laid her hand on Karen's. "You don't need to worry. Anyone can tell that man cares deeply for you."

Karen resumed stitching the hem of Clay's shirt, dearly wanting to believe what her friend said. But Clay had been gone from Arcadia for years and had sent her precious few letters during that time. After Aunt Alice died, she thought she could live well in the house her aunt had left her, but then she discovered that Aunt Alice owed hundreds of dollars in back taxes and other debts. Once the house was sold and the debts paid, there wouldn't be much left.

When she explained the situation to Clay's mother, the kind woman had offered to let her live with them, but Karen didn't want to accept charity. If only she had some skill with which she could support herself. The day she received Clay's telegram, asking her to marry him, she'd thought her problems were over. She agreed to wed because of their strong friendship and because she'd cared for him for a long while. But was he merely offering her another form of charity, because as a pastor he needed a wife, or did he truly want to marry her?

But hadn't he proved that point? Even stated it out loud?

Karen hated that her father's abandonment made it hard for her to trust. But if she couldn't trust Clay, who could she trust?

She sighed, frustrated with her confusion. Clay had

always been a cherished friend and had treated her with kindness. He'd been the one to make her laugh for the first time after her father left. He'd been a confidant with whom she'd shared her deepest hurts—the brother she never had. But now she wanted him to be more. The man who loved and cherished her—her husband. So why was she doubting him? Had she allowed the needling voice of the enemy to cause her to distrust her best friend and his good intentions?

"I hate to go, but I reckon I oughta start fixin' supper." Patsy rose and gave her a quick hug. "Don't worry about that man of yours."

Karen closed the door after Patsy left and walked to the window. Before coming to Bakerstown, she'd spent several weeks deciding what to take with her and what to sell. Clay's mother had helped, but one day she showed up with some of Karen's friends, announcing that Karen needed a trousseau, so they'd switched gears and started sewing. Since her arrival, she'd been busy with Clay and finishing her sewing projects. A long time had passed since she'd spent time reading the Bible and praying regularly. Was it possible that marrying Clay was not God's will for her life? In all her hustle and bustle, had she moved forward with her own dreams and left God behind?

On Sunday morning, Karen sat in church waiting for Clay to enter. Would he wear the shirt she'd given him last night? His surprised and pleased expression when she presented it to him had warmed her heart, as had the gift he'd given her—a pine-green apron with an embroidered bib sporting a cardinal. If he kept surprising her with gifts, she might soon become spoiled, although she secretly enjoyed them. Her aunt had always given her a birthday present and something at Christmas, but no one had ever given her random gifts before, and she cherished them even though they were practical.

A commotion to her left drew her gaze to the aisle, where Patsy halted with a tall, thin man. "Can we sit with you?"

Karen smiled. "Of course." She slid over to make room for the couple.

Patsy scooted in, followed by her husband. She yanked on his arm. "This here's Pastor Parsons's fiancée that I been tellin' you about." She turned to Karen, beaming with pride. "This here's my Jared."

"I'm happy to meet you," Karen said.

Jared nodded, the skin above his neatly trimmed beard turning red.

Patsy leaned toward her, eyes gleaming. "So, did you give Pastor the shirt?"

"I did, and he seemed quite thrilled with it."

"Did he wear it?"

Karen shrugged. "I haven't seen him. He likes to spend Sunday morning praying and studying."

The pianist took her seat and began the opening song. The chattering around the sanctuary quieted as everyone sat down and turned their attention toward the front. Clay stepped in through the side door and took his place behind the lectern, his gaze immediately seeking her out. He smiled then glanced around the room at the others. "Will you all rise and join me in song this bright Sunday morning?"

Delight soared through Karen to see the vivid white shirt she'd painstakingly stitched peeking out above Clay's waistcoat. She sat a bit straighter, glad she was finally mastering the art of sewing. Clay's mother would be proud.

He cleared his throat. "Mrs. Willard, would you please come forward and give today's announcements?" He stepped back, rolled his shoulders, and tugged on one of his sleeves.

Helen, who sat on the second aisle, stood and hurried forward. "As you all know, next Saturday evening, we'll have our annual Christmas sing-along and auction to raise money for the Buckner Orphans Home in Dallas." She cocked her head. "My daughter, Prudence, will be making several of her famous rhubarb pies, so I know you unmarried men will be eager to bid."

Karen was pretty sure Jared snorted—or maybe he had something caught in his throat. Either way, he received an elbow in his side, courtesy of his wife.

Helen continued, "I do hope all you ladies will be as generous as you have in the past to support this worthy cause. This auction helps the orphanage to provide the children with hearty meals. And don't forget the very special Christmas Eve service a week from Thursday and the wedding that follows of our own Pastor Parsons and Karen Briggs."

Clay stepped forward, again tugging on his sleeve. Karen felt the blood rush from her face. Had she forgotten to remove some pins?

"Thank you, Mrs. Willard. I haven't had the pleasure of sampling the fares of the bake sale, but I look forward to it."

He glanced down at his sleeve and frowned. Karen stared at it, and her heart skipped a beat. If she wasn't mistaken, the cuff hung further out from the end of his coat sleeve than it had before.

"If you have your Bible with you, please open it to, uh. . ." Clay rolled his right shoulder then stared at his cuff, eyebrows dipped. He gave it another tug and pulled the sleeve out a full two inches. He lifted his questioning gaze toward Karen.

She slid down on the bench, using the man's head in front of her to block her view of her fiancé. What had she done wrong?

Patsy leaned over. "Looks as if Pastor's got a problem. You did remember to stitch in the sleeve and didn't just leave it basted?"

Karen flicked a glance at her friend as she felt the blood drain from her face. Had she forgotten that step in her haste to finish before she and Clay had dinner last night?

Clay chuckled. "Pardon the distraction, folks. It seems I'm having garment troubles today."

Face burning, Karen hunkered down on the bench, praying no one had overheard Patsy's loud whisper about her making the shirt. Why, oh why had she thought she could tackle such a project? Even on her best day, she'd never been a good seamstress. But Clay needed a shirt so badly—and he'd given her so much.

Patsy rose, and Karen realized she hadn't heard a single word of Clay's sermon. She stood on shaky legs, hoping to make a quick getaway and not talk to anyone.

She dared to peek at Clay, and the horrid sleeve now covered his fingertips. As he talked to a man who'd sat on the front row, he surreptitiously folded the cuff in half so that it didn't look so bad.

As soon as Patsy stepped into the aisle and moved aside, Karen squeezed into the crowd, making her way to the back door. She was supposed to have dinner with Clay, but at the moment, she couldn't bear to see him. No matter what she did, she was a failure.

Chapter 6

Karen wished she could ignore the knocking on her door, but she couldn't abide being rude. She swiped her eyes and pinched her cheeks then opened the door. Fragrant aromas from downstairs drifted in the door, making her stomach gurgle in spite of her lack of appetite.

Mrs. Grady lifted one brow. "Must have been one troubling message the pastor preached."

A tiny smile tugged at one corner of Karen's mouth. "It's not that. I'm surprised you haven't heard what happened yet."

"Tell me later. Gotta get our Sunday dinner dished up, and the pastor is waiting in the parlor for you."

"I don't suppose you could tell him I'm not feeling well?"

The landlady's expression sobered. "You're sick?"

Karen shrugged. "Truthfully, no. Just sick at heart."

"Did that charming rascal do something untoward?"

"No! No. Nothing like that." She glanced away,

feeling her cheeks warming again. She sighed. She had to face up to what she did and explain what happened.

Mrs. Grady's eyes widened as Karen told her about the sleeve slipping down Clay's arm. Then she burst out in a belly laugh.

"It's not funny." Karen frowned and crossed her arms. "I'm humiliated."

Tears glistened in the older woman's eyes. "I'm sorry, but that's the most amusing tale I've heard in a long while." She patted Karen's shoulder and wiped a tear from the corner of her eye. "Remind me to tell you about the first shirt I made for Mr. Grady." She turned and bustled toward the stairs, still chuckling.

Karen hurried over and peered into the mirror, not liking what she saw. Her face was splotchy, her eyes puffy, and her nose red. She didn't want Clay to see her like this, but there was nothing to be done about it. She could hardly keep him waiting until her complexion returned to normal.

Downstairs she paused at the entrance to the parlor. Clay stood at the window, looking out. He'd changed from her shirt to a plaid one. She couldn't blame him for wanting to remove that dreadful thing. He must have heard her, because he turned and smiled. "I looked for you after church."

Karen ducked her head, afraid any sympathy on his part would set her crying again. Why couldn't he be angry? It would make her feel better.

He crossed the room and stopped in front of her. "Are you all right?"

She shrugged but didn't look up.

"Tell me what's wrong."

"Surely you know. I sat through the whole service, watching your sleeve slide farther and farther down your arm."

He chuckled. "That was unexpected. I wasn't quite sure what was happening. I thought maybe I'd torn it off with all of my tugging."

A ray of hope pushed away her misery. Could his tugging have caused the sleeve to come loose? "Why *were* you pulling on it?"

His eyes widened, and his ears turned red. "Uh. . .it's a very nice shirt."

"You don't have to spare my feelings. I know something was wrong."

"Uh. . .well. . .it pinched my underarm a bit."

"Oh. I should have made it bigger."

His taut expression eased. "When we're married, you'll be able to try things on me before you finish them so you can adjust them if needed."

Karen snorted and looked away. "You're such an optimist, Clay. I don't know as I'll ever attempt to make you another item of clothing."

He took her hands. "I hope you do. It's a fine shirt. It just needs a few adjustments. Even when I buy ready-made shirts, they sometimes need tweaking."

It was impossible to stay angry in light of his encouragement. "Tweaking—as in needing a new sleeve?"

He grinned. "Well, maybe not a whole sleeve, but sometimes they need to be shortened or the buttons moved."

"I'm mortified. Everyone must think I'm a buffoon."

He took hold of her shoulders. "Karen, no one even knows you made the shirt, so how could they think that?"

She shrugged. Perhaps he was right. Once again she was making a mountain out of a molehill.

"Dinner's ready," Mrs. Grady called from the dining room.

Footsteps sounded upstairs as the other boarders made their way across the hall and down the stairs.

"Better put on a smile, or those other boarders will be booting me out the door, thinking I did something to upset you."

In spite of her misery, a smile lifted her lips.

"That's my girl." He glanced past her then dipped

down, stealing a kiss and setting her heart dancing. "Stop worrying so much. I love the shirt and hope you'll make the needed adjustments once we're married."

"Just don't blame me if it falls apart again."

He chuckled. "All right. I'll lay the blame on Mrs. Willard."

A giggle bubbled up and spilled out. "Shame on you, Pastor."

He winked then looped her arm through his and escorted her into the dining room. This was the Clay she remembered—the one who could always make her feel better, no matter the situation. The only man other than her father whom she had ever loved.

∞

Karen deposited the last of the half-dozen fruitcakes she'd made for the auction on the crowded table, feeling a bit proud of how nicely they'd turned out. At least her cooking skills couldn't be questioned.

"Those turned out lovely. After smelling them baking all afternoon, I just might have to purchase one." Mrs. Grady leaned over and sniffed. "Mmm. . ."

Karen lifted her hand to her mouth. "Oh my, I should have thought to make you one. It was so kind of you to allow me to use your kitchen and some of your supplies."

Mrs. Grady swatted her hand in the air. "You saved me some extra work. I always attend the auction and donate something. It's for a worthy cause. And my donating supplies while you did the baking worked out well."

Clay walked up to them. "I sure hope you made one of those for me. How long has it been since I tasted your scrumptious fruitcake?"

Karen smiled, inwardly delighted. "Probably the Christmas before last. But if you want one now, you'll have to buy it. This is all I baked."

Clay stroked his chin, a mischievous expression on his handsome face. "I just might have to do that." He glanced around the crowded room. "Although, with all the people here, the competition should be quite stiff."

Karen patted his arm. "Have no fears. If you don't get one today, I'll make a special one for you after we're married."

"I'll look forward to that."

Mrs. Willard and two other women halted on the opposite side of the table, followed by Prudy, who looked as if she'd been chewing on fresh rhubarb. Karen couldn't help admiring her lovely, dark green velvet dress.

"Looks like we'll be making another fine donation to

the Buckner Orphans Home this year." Helen Willard's gaze swung along the four tables filled with sweet-smelling baked goods. "It was kind of you to donate six fruitcakes, Mrs. Grady."

"Oh, they're mostly from Miss Briggs. I just provided some of the supplies and my kitchen. Karen did the baking."

Helen lifted her chin but managed a somewhat grateful look. "How kind of you, Miss Briggs, with you so new to town and all." Her gaze swiveled away. "Pastor, did you happen to see that Prudence baked *eight* rhubarb pies?"

Rue-barb was more like it. Karen crossed her arms, feeling the poke of the woman's barb and her pride that her daughter had donated more than Karen had.

"They look mighty tasty, Mrs. Willard, but I have to say, I prefer cake to pies."

Karen straightened. Bless Clay's heart.

Mrs. Willard harrumphed then moved down the table, most likely searching for other victims to lord her daughter's efforts over.

Prudy stared down at the fruitcakes. "They look absolutely delicious. What all do you put in them?"

Karen relaxed. Had Prudy finally decided to be civil? "Um. . .well, besides the basics like flour and sugar, I add raisins, currants, mace, nutmeg, and candied lemons and cherries."

Prudy's brow dipped, and she tapped one finger against her mouth. "You don't use brandy in it? I was certain I spied you buying a bottle at the mercantile. Surely you don't drink the stuff."

"Of course she doesn't." Clay straightened, obviously upset by Prudy's accusation. "How could you ask such a thing?"

Mrs. Willard and her cronies moved back toward her and Clay.

Karen's face flamed. Some women took offense to brandy being used in fruitcakes, so she'd refrained from mentioning it. "I do use it, because the brandy keeps the cakes from molding and prolongs their life. But I merely soak the raisins in it. The potency cooks out, so you can't even tell it's there."

Gasps surrounded her. Prudy glowed proud, but her mother's face paled. "You put liquor in your fruitcakes?" Lois Clemmons fanned her face with her hand.

Karen stared at the floor, wishing she was an insect and could crawl under the table. She'd tried to do something nice—something to support the church's event—but once again she failed.

"Now, Lois, don't make such a stink. Using brandy

for baking is quite common." Mrs. Grady sent Karen a smile.

Karen backed away from the table, fearing she may well have cost Clay his job. All around her, the crowd pressed in and people grumbled. She spun. "Excuse me, please. I need some air."

"Karen. Wait!" Clay called out, but she continued squeezing through the throng.

She pushed her way outside then ran all the way back to the boardinghouse. It was no use. She was the wrong bride for Clay, and it was time he faced the facts.

Chapter 7

Clay longed to go after Karen—to soothe the wounds the church ladies had carelessly inflicted—but he had responsibilities here. Everyone seemed to be talking at once. He lifted two fingers to his mouth and whistled. The noise quieted instantly, and everyone looked at him. "Let's not forget this is a church event, even if we are not in the church. Please quiet down, and we'll begin the auction. Where's Elmer?"

"Back here, Parson Parsons. Let me through, folks. I'm the auctioneer."

"Everyone knows that, Elmer." Fred Smith chuckled, as did half the crowd.

Clay relaxed as the tension of the crowd eased, but there was still one person he had to confront. He searched for Prudy and was not surprised to see her making her way toward him, smiling like a child who'd stolen a pie from a window sill.

She batted her long lashes at him. "I'm so sorry, Clay. I had no idea that the mention of brandy would upset everyone."

He crossed his arms, fighting hard not to lose control. "Lying doesn't become you, Miss Willard. I know exactly what you were doing. And it won't work."

She pouted and swirled her skirts, obviously struggling to maintain an innocent gaze. "What won't work?"

"Trying to chase Karen away. She's the woman I intend to marry, and if it means leaving my church to do so, I will."

She paled. "Why would you want that mouse when you could have me? I've practically thrown myself at you. Any other man would have married me months ago."

Clay shook his head, feeling sorry for the woman. "You don't understand. Karen has owned my heart for more than a decade. There is no other woman for me."

She ducked her head. He hated hurting her, but she had to stop chasing after him and pestering Karen.

A ruckus behind him drew his attention. Bart Tremble waved a dollar in the air. "Start with them fruitcakes. I want one."

"Me, too." Silas Hightower stepped in front of Bart. "I'll bid two dollars."

"Three!"

Clay looked up front at Mrs. Willard's stunned face and smiled. It looked as if Karen's fruitcakes were a winner—at least with the men. He turned back, and Prudy was gone. Good. He needed to find Karen and tell her the good news.

⌐∞

What a mess she'd made of things. Karen slapped a blouse into her satchel but then jumped at a knock on her bedroom door. As far as she knew, she was alone in the house.

"Open the door, Karen."

Clay. She didn't want to see him—to break his heart. "Go away."

"I'm not leaving, so you might as well open the door."

Sighing, she did as ordered. "You shouldn't be here. If anyone found out—"

"I don't care what anyone thinks." He stepped into her room, eyes beseeching her to believe him. "I love you. I should have told you years ago, but I wanted to get settled—to have a home for us first."

Karen shook her head. "It's too late. I can't be the wife you need. I'm leaving, Clay."

"Leaving! You don't mean that. Where will you go?"

She shrugged and turned back to the open satchel on her bed. "I'm sorry, but I won't be the cause of you losing your church."

"I can get another church, but you're the only woman for me. Can't you see that? I've loved you for as long as I can remember."

She shook her head. She loved him too much to bring about his demise. "I'm sorry. But it won't work."

He stepped closer. "Karen—"

Steeling herself, she spun around. Better to hurt him now than later. She held up her hand. "I'm not changing my mind."

His deep sigh and sad eyes were almost her undoing.

"Fine. I won't force you to marry me." He spun around and was gone.

≈

Clay walked down Main Street, confusion warring within him. He thought marrying Karen was God's will, but had his love for her overruled his ability to hear God on the subject?

Silas Hightower moseyed toward him, holding one of Karen's fruitcakes and chewing. He slowed as he neared Clay. "This is the best stuff I've ever eaten. You'd be a fool, Pastor, not to marry a woman who can cook like her."

The man's comment didn't help his crumpled emotions. As much as he wanted to head home, hide out, and nurse his wounded heart, he needed to check on things—and the Christmas sing-along was to start soon. He was expected to get it going, but then maybe he could sneak out after that.

Clay returned to the building where the auction was being held and scanned the table. Most of the items had already been claimed. Mrs. Willard spied him and moved in his direction. She was the next-to-last person he wanted to talk with now. He backed out the door, ready to tuck tail and run.

"Pastor, wait. Please."

Her contrite tone slowed his steps, and he turned. Helen approached, along with her sister and Lois Clemmons. Helen cleared her throat. "We'd like to apologize."

"It's my fault." Lois ducked her head. "My father was a drunkard, and I can't abide alcohol. But I do feel we overreacted and owe Miss Briggs an apology."

"I agree. You'll find her at the boardinghouse."

Lois nodded, and she and Loraine turned that way.

Helen moved closer. "Pastor, I do hope you won't hold any hard feelings against Prudence. She's a woman scorned and was desperate to gain your attention."

Clay crossed his arms. "Your daughter's games hurt a good woman and may have jeopardized our marriage.

I forgive her, but I also made it clear that I am not now, nor have I ever been, interested in her as a potential wife. Karen is the only woman for me."

Helen ducked her head and nodded. "I understand. She won't bother you again."

Clay watched her hurry to catch up with the other two women, feeling only marginally better. It was good the women were on their way to apologize. He probably ought to be there—just in case. First, he had to get something from his home—one last gift.

❦

Persistent knocking at the front door drew Karen from her room. She didn't want to answer, but it might be a prospective boarder, and she wouldn't be the cause of Mrs. Grady losing business.

She opened the door, stunned to see the trio responsible for her latest woes.

Lois quickly explained and apologized.

"And we want you to know we're sincerely happy to have you here in Bakerstown," Mrs. Willard said.

Loraine nodded. "You make Pastor Clay happy."

Karen's chilled heart began to thaw. "Thank you so much for coming. You can't know how much it means."

The women left as quickly as they came, but a foot slid into the opening before she could close the door.

She stepped back, and Clay pushed into the room.

She crossed her arms. "Why are you back?"

"Because I can't let you leave. We belong together—we always have. This is for you." He held out a package—too small to be something for her kitchen.

"Clay. . ."

"Please. Just open it."

Even though she knew she shouldn't, Karen unwrapped the paper and opened the tiny box. She gasped. A beautiful ring with a blue sapphire gleamed in the light shining through the door. "Oh Clay. It's lovely."

He stepped forward. "I love you, Karen. Please don't go. Stay and be my wife."

Leaving him was wrong. She knew it. All it would create was misery for them both. She loved this man and didn't want to live without him. Tears coursing down her face, she nodded.

Clay smiled and took her into his arms. "Oh sweetheart, you don't know how happy that makes me. I love you so much."

"I love you, too, and I promise never to make another fruitcake."

Clay threw back his head and laughed. When he finally stopped, he captured her gaze. "I certainly hope that's one promise you don't keep."

⬥

Late Christmas Eve, Clay lifted Karen off the porch and carried her through the door of the parsonage—their home. He kicked the door shut then claimed her lips, kissing her as he'd longed to do for years.

After a while, Karen pulled back, gleaming in the love of a newly married woman. "I have a gift for you."

"Oh you do?" He grinned.

"It's not what you're thinking. Please put me down."

Reluctantly, he set her on her feet. She opened the satchel he'd placed on the table earlier and pulled out a box and handed it to him.

Curious, he lifted the lid, delighted at the fruity aroma that greeted him. "A fruitcake!"

Karen smiled.

He set the cake on the table then waggled his brows. "I'd love some later, but right now, I prefer to enjoy my wife—and she's much sweeter than fruitcake."

Fruit Cake by Measure

2 scant teacupfuls butter
3 cupfuls dark brown sugar
Half a grated nutmeg
1 tablespoon ground
  cinnamon
1 teaspoon ground cloves
1 teaspoon mace
½ cupful molasses
½ cupful sour milk
6 eggs, whites and yolks
  beaten separately

1 cupful lemon and/or orange
  juice
4 cupfuls sifted flour
1 level teaspoon baking soda
1 pound raisins, seeded
Currants, washed and dried
½ pound citron, cut in
  thin strips

Cream butter and sugar; add nutmeg, cinnamon, and cloves; add molasses and sour milk. Stir well; then add egg yolks and juice; stir again thoroughly. Add flour alternately with the egg whites. Dissolve baking soda and stir in thoroughly. Mix fruit together, and stir into it 2 heaping tablespoons flour; then stir it in the cake batter. Butter two baking pans carefully, line them with parchment, well buttered, and bake at 350 degrees for 2 hours. After it is baked, let cake cool in the pans. Afterward, put in an airtight container, or cover tightly in the pans.

Mrs. S. A. Camp, Grand Rapids, Michigan

About the Author

Bestselling author Vickie McDonough grew up wanting to marry a rancher, but instead she married a computer geek who is scared of horses. She now lives out her dreams in her fictional stories about ranchers, cowboys, lawmen, and others living in the West during the 1800s. Vickie is the award-winning author of more than thirty published books and novellas. Her books include the fun and feisty Texas Boardinghouse Brides series and *End of the Trail*, which was the Oklahoma Writers' Federation, Inc., 2013 Best Fiction Novel winner. Her *Whispers on the Prairie* was a *Romantic Times* Recommended Inspirational Book for July 2013. Vickie has been married for thirty-nine years. She has four grown sons and one daughter-in-law, and is grandma to a feisty eight-year-old girl. When she's not writing, Vickie enjoys reading, antiquing, watching movies, and traveling. To learn more about Vickie's books or to sign up for her newsletter, visit her website: www.vickiemcdonough.com.

Coming Soon from
Barbour Books. . .

Christmas Wedding Bells

Available wherever books are sold.